Considering that it was her sister who had had an illegitimate baby and then walked out on it and the baby's father, leaving Naomi to cope, it seemed particularly unfair that as a result Naomi's own boy-friend Gareth Gill assumed it was *her* baby and rejected her accordingly! Why didn't anyone take her side?

Books you will enjoy
by LILIAN PEAKE

NIGHT OF POSSESSION

Holiday romances don't often lead to anything more serious—and Lisa's encounter with Zander Cameron in the Canary Islands didn't even really come under the heading of 'holiday romance'—so she had even less reason to expect anything to come of it. Which was just as well . . .

NO OTHER MAN

It had been concern for her mother, and no other reason, that had made Suzanne refuse to go abroad with Ross Beckett whom she had loved so dearly—but as a result, he had left her in anger and bitterness and she had not seen him since. Now, six years later, he was back. But how could she ever expect him to forgive her.

ACROSS A CROWDED ROOM (Best Seller)

Lisette was struggling to keep the family business going against overwhelming odds—but it looked as if soon she was going to have to admit defeat. One man could help her—Rosco Hamden—but his price would be a high one. Could she bring herself to pay it?

PASSIONATE INTRUDER

'No man is an island,' Sharon Mason had reminded Calum Caldar—to which he had replied firmly, 'This man is.' So she had better not let herself fall in love with him, had she? Especially as he persisted in believing all those lying stories about her . . .

COME LOVE ME

BY

LILIAN PEAKE

MILLS & BOON LIMITED
15-16 BROOK'S MEWS
LONDON W1A 1DR

All the characters in this book have no existence outside the imagination of the Author, and have no relation whatsoever to anyone bearing the same name or names. They are not even distantly inspired by any individual known or unknown to the Author, and all the incidents are pure invention.

The text of this publication or any part thereof may not be reproduced or transmitted in any form or by any means, electronic or mechanical, including photocopying, recording, storage in an information retrieval system, or otherwise, without the written permission of the publisher.

This book is sold subject to the condition that it shall not, by way of trade or otherwise, be lent, resold, hired out or otherwise circulated without the prior consent of the publisher in any form of binding or cover other than that in which it is published and without a similar condition including this condition being imposed on the subsequent purchaser.

First published 1983
Australian copyright 1983
Philippine copyright 1984
This edition 1984

© Lilian Peake 1983

ISBN 0 263 74483 3

Set in Monophoto Plantin 10 on 11 pt.
01–0284 – 53870

Made and printed in Great Britain by
Richard Clay (The Chaucer Press) Ltd,
Bungay, Suffolk

Another for Lewis
with my love

CHAPTER ONE

'THERE'S your little daughter,' Naomi remarked, handing over the sweet-smelling, bathed and night-gowned four-month-old to her father.

There was the same pleasure and pride on the young man's face as there had been from the moment he had been allowed to see his newborn baby daughter.

'You know,' Brian commented, not for the first time, 'there's a distinct look of you about her.' He held the sleepy bundle against him and inspected the miniature features.

Naomi shook her head. 'It's no use fooling yourself. Becky's not mine, nor am I Clare. You won't get any silly ideas in your head, will you, about me taking Clare's place permanently?'

Alarm pleated his forehead. 'That's not the introduction to your usual speech reminding me you've got a life of your own to live? For heaven's sake, Naomi, where would I be without you?'

'I'll tell you where, even if I am repeating myself. You'd have to give up your job as a carpenter, and stay at home to look after Becky. You'd be tied to the house or you'd have to take her everywhere you go. To the pub, to parties . . .'

'Okay, okay!' He held up his hand, then quickly replaced it to support the baby. His pale blue eyes held defiance, plus a deep-down pain. 'You've forgotten something. I'd have to take her with me evenings, when I'd do odd jobs for people to help keep my daughter fed and properly clothed.'

Naomi sighed, pushing her shoulder-length dark

brown hair from her cheeks. 'I may sound monotonous, Brian, but it's all true, isn't it? Anyway, you played your part in producing that little bundle, as well as my sister.'

'Look——' he had spoken loudly, making the half-asleep baby stir. 'Look,' he went on more quietly, 'she told me it was okay, because she——'

Naomi nodded. 'Clare always has been careless about important things. Plus thoughtless.'

'Thoughtless?' Brian spoke bitterly now. 'Thoughtless, when she had it all planned out? She stayed for nearly three months, then walked out on us.' He looked down at his daughter. 'Leaving *her*, let alone me! She'd been offered a part in a play in the north-west. It could lead eventually to a television appearance, she said. Good for you, I told her. Right, so you're putting selfish gain before human needs—two human's needs.'

Naomi rose, straightening her dress and brushing her skirt free of talc. 'Surely you knew Clare well enough to realise that nothing you said would make her change her mind once it was made up? Why didn't you marry her, then she might have felt under some obligation.'

'Do you think I didn't ask her? Once I knew about the baby coming, I tried everything to make her marry me, but she had all the answers ready.'

'We're going round in circles, Brian.' Naomi looked at her watch. 'Sure you can manage to put her to bed? Fine. I'll go, then.'

'Down to Sussex, to your parents?'

Naomi nodded. 'Nowhere else for me to go, is there?'

Brian looked up at her with sympathy. 'No word from your boy-friend?'

'Nothing. He's keeping to his list of rules. No letters, no phone calls, no meetings.'

'You don't half sound bitter! Anyway, he must have been mad, not coming down once to see you.' He smiled and there was a trace of envy in his tone. 'You look great in that green ribbed thing and that black skirt. Whew, what a figure! You're almost as good as Clare.'

Naomi laughed at his praise, qualified though it was. 'Don't you dare start substituting me for your runaway partner and the mother of your child! We might look alike just a bit, but in personality——'

'I was an idiot, wasn't I? I should have fallen for you, not her.'

'I know.' Naomi turned from the door. 'I'm the sensible one, with brains plus a sense of duty, all of which Clare hasn't got. But for you, she's got something else.'

Brian was shaking his head, his eyes on his baby as she lay in his arms. 'I still can't understand how your boy-friend could cut himself off from you like he has.'

'He wanted to marry me, he said, but he wanted *me* to be absolutely sure. I'm nine years younger than he is. He said it would give me a chance to get myself another boy-friend, if I wanted.'

Brian looked up, immediately interested. 'Naomi——?'

Naomi smiled sadly into the young, flushed face, the features sharp with the burden of worry which had been placed so firmly on his shoulders by her own callous sister. 'Not a chance, Brian. Sorry.'

Brian stared into his tiny daughter's face, saying nothing.

Naomi gazed through the glass of the patio doors at the rear of her parents' living-room, looking at the well-tended garden.

Her parents had gone out. Their greeting, when she had arrived, had been warm and welcoming. She was aware they were making an extra fuss of her because of the unselfish way she had given up her secretarial job at the university to take Clare's place.

It was lonely, she found, with no one to talk to. If her mother had been there, she would have talked the whole time about her unofficial granddaughter. Naomi discovered that, alone as she was, having an evening and night free of the responsibilities of looking after someone else's error was not the pleasure she had anticipated.

Her thoughts would keep returning to the baby, wondering how Brian was coping, whether he would wake up if the baby cried in the night. If so, would he know what to do?

Inside her, there was a residue of bitterness towards her sister. They had been born of the same parents. The same blood ran in their veins, yet she could not have done what Clare had done, coldly and calculatedly. When Gareth came back—she did not even know the exact date—what should she do? It was a question she had asked herself over and over again.

A sense of imprisonment, of being walled in, overcame her. She released the catch on the patio door and stepped outside on to the paving stones. There was a compulsion inside her to get into the open air. She recognised it as a kind of escape mechanism.

Her impatient feet took her to the end of the long garden, through the growing beds of vegetables and as far as the boundary fence. On the way back, she inhaled the increasing heaviness of the evening air.

It was such an evening that Gareth Gill had gone away. At the time the two years they would be spending apart had seemed an eternity. It had, in fact become a nightmare of days leading to dreams of being in Gareth's arms, only to wake and find herself alone. And there were still at least three months to go.

The evening they had said goodbye, Gareth had

driven her into the countryside. They had wandered along their favourite path which took them through a wood. She had been nineteen, Gareth twenty-eight.

'You're still too young to commit yourself,' Gareth had told her firmly. 'The two years I'm away will be a time of testing.'

'My love for you doesn't need testing,' she had protested, facing him and pulling at the sleeves of his sweater.

He had run a finger down her neat nose, shaking his head. 'There aren't any doubts in my mind. But I'm determined our marriage will last, which is why I want *you* to be as sure as I am.' He had kissed her deeply. 'Understand me, Naomi?'

'No, I don't understand,' she had replied with desperation. 'I know *now* that I want to marry you. Two whole years——' She had turned her face into his neck. 'How will I live that long without you?'

He had laughed. 'You'll find a way. And another thing.' He had pinched her chin hard. 'It won't be easy, but it'll leave you free.'

Naomi had frowned. 'Free? Of what? You? I don't want to be free of you.' She had stared into his unmoved grey eyes. 'You're not going to suggest we don't even write to each other?'

'That's just what I was going to say. No letters, no phone calls, nothing. It will give you the freedom to get yourself another boy-friend, if that's what you decide you want.'

'I don't want another boy-friend,' she had cried. 'I only want you—*you*!'

He had pulled her down to the hard ground. They were out of sight of the path and deep in the woods. 'Oh, God,' he had said softly, as though the full impact of what he had just suggested had hit him, 'it will be hell. My love, I want you, want you . . .'

'Take me, darling,' she had whispered, her hands

clinging to him. 'It'll be a bond, a seal. If—if you make love to me now, I think I might—just—be able to bear those two years without you.'

There had been only a little daylight left, a soft glow with which the trees, in their swaying, had played hide-and-seek. His eyes had searched hers and he had pulled her against him. 'You know what you're saying?'

She had nodded and felt all his muscles tighten to a thrusting hardness. She sensed that he was holding his breath, then he released it. 'To hell with rules,' he had muttered, and tore off his shirt, throwing it aside.

He had undressed her slowly, knowing of her inexperience and respecting it. His lips had kissed her to a gripping, radiant life, his knowing hands caressing, pressing and lingering, until she had cried out to feel the pressure of his skin against hers.

Afterwards, they had lain, cheek against flushed cheek, hearing in the wood's deep silence the throbbing of their own hearts. Naomi had felt the brush of his eyelashes as his eyes had come open, seeking and finding in hers a reflection of his own pleasure and happiness.

'Now I belong to you for ever,' she had murmured against his cheek, Gareth had smiled and taken a possessive kiss. Wanting him to speak with words as well as actions, she had persisted, 'There's no need to test my love for you, darling. Haven't I just shown you how very much I love you?' He had placed a smiling kiss on the end of her nose. Impatient for him to reciprocate by telling of his love for her, she had nudged, 'Or is it really *your* love you want to put to the test?'

His eyes had grown so cold, she had shivered. He had gripped her arms. 'Say you're sorry for that remark, or I'll——' He had not needed to finish the sentence.

'I'm sorry, Gareth,' she had interrupted quickly. 'Now you can smile at me again, can't you?'

'Minx,' he had muttered against her lips. He had held her breast gently, as if it were precious and he must have felt the coldness of her flesh. Moving quickly, he had freed her. 'Dress yourself, you shameless female,' he had joked, rising and pulling on his own clothes.

Naomi re-entered her parents' living-room, closing the doors and securing them as if the past was still out there. It was not the loving she had wanted to exclude, but the terrible moments of parting.

There was the high-pitched ring of the telephone from the entrance hall. Answering it, she found herself saying, 'No, I'm not Mrs Pemberton. Mum's out. I'm her daughter. No, I'm not Clare, I'm the younger one, Naomi.'

'Well, I know I haven't spoken to your mother for a year or two,' came the woman's laughing answer, 'but I didn't believe she could possibly have such a young voice! I'm Betty Higgins, by the way. You might not remember me. I've been abroad with my husband for a year or so. Just thought I might have a chat with her. Never mind. You'll tell her I rang, won't you?'

Naomi agreed at once that she would tell her mother and, with relief, ended the conversation. She had been in no mood to be chatty to her mother's friends. Anyone more gossipy might have probed.

Clare's callousness and stupidity were forbidden subjects, strictly not to be discussed outside the family. Which meant that her own activities were banned, too, except that she no longer lived at home.

Yes, she would have had to say, I'm down from London for the night. Oh, it's not bad, really, living there. Much noisier than here in Sussex, of course. Yes, when I'm in London I do miss the slower pace of these lovely country villages, but . . .

The telephone shrilled before she had taken more than a few steps from it. She almost decided to let it ring itself out, feeling that by taking one call for her mother, she had already done her duty, but before she knew what she was about, instinct made her hand reach out.

'Pemberton's residence,' she answered, adding before the caller had a chance to speak, 'I'm sorry, my mother and father are out——'

'But you're not.'

The voice was deep, amused and intensely masculine. Her heart leapt crazily. 'You?' was all she could manage, too choked with pleasure to tell him how happy it made her just to hear him speaking. Faintly, she could discern that his breath was coming faster, almost caressing her ear. 'You're breaking your own rule!'

'To hell with rules.' He repeated the words he had used that evening they had made passionate love in the woods. This time, however, he had spoken with a kind of anger, not with eager abandonment as he had before.

His sharpness made her realise too late that her welcome, after so long an absence, was totally inadequate, but it was all she could think of to say.

Trying to make amends, she went on, 'Couldn't you wait——' Like me, she had been going to add, but he answered too quickly.

'Why, would you rather I had?' His tone had gone as dry as the tiny fragments of history he had been uncovering at the archaeological site in York where he had been working for so long.

Desperate to put matters right between them, she let the eagerness take over. 'Gareth darling, if only you knew how much I've longed to hear from you!'

There was a small silence, then he said dryly, 'It sounds as if you've been learning a part.'

'If only you were here, I could *show* you,' she blurted out, pushing at her hair and finding that her hand was trembling. 'Anyway,' she counter-attacked now, 'did you only phone me to be—to be——' Her voice was shaking and she couldn't go on.

His breathing was uneven as he broke in, 'Naomi, the last thing I wanted was to upset you.' His voice had deepened with emotion. 'It's true I couldn't wait. I told myself that all I wanted was to talk to you, hear you speak. It's not enough—I want to see you. It's been hellish these months away from you. Come north, Naomi, come to me——'

It was difficult, she found, speaking over her tears. 'Oh, Gareth, I'd love to, but——' It was impossible to go on.

'But——?' He was drifting out of her reach again. There was a frightening silence, then he asked in a tone which chilled her through, 'What's stopping you?'

Brian had pleaded, holding his daughter close, 'Don't tell anyone about what's happened, Naomi. Keep what Clare did a secret between us—and your parents, of course.' She had given her promise to do as he had asked.

'I can't explain, Gareth.' It almost choked her to say the words.

'You mean not on the telephone? Then come to York and tell me.'

'I can't, Gareth, I can't get away.' She was whispering now.

His only response was a deadly silence, more terrifying than the other two put together. It was time to let her heart speak, otherwise, instinct told her, she might never see him again. 'I—I want you to make love to me, Gareth. I want your arms around me like you held me before.' She swallowed back the catch in her throat. 'But I can't, darling, I just can't!'

The crash of the receiver from the other end told her he had gone.

Naomi did not see her parents until breakfast time next day. Even so, she only heard her father as he called, 'Hello, dear, goodbye.' He was off to work, and Naomi, at the top of the stairs, laughed.

'See you next time I come, Dad,' she called. The door closed as he hurried off.

'I'll be down soon,' she told her mother, then hastened to finish her dressing. Inspecting her face, she saw the shadows of a restless night lingering around her eyes.

They told a tale of hours of useless thinking, of trying to find a solution to an insoluble problem. The sound of Gareth's voice, too, hadn't left her alone. He had broken his own rule by phoning her, impelled by his apparent need to make contact. Yet somehow, instead of being the pleasure it should have been, it had been a disaster.

The image of his face as she remembered it had kept coming at her through the darkness like a television close-up, every detail picked out. There was his brown hair with its intriguing red lights inherited, he had told her, from his mother. It had taken him a long time to tell her, also, that his mother had divorced his father and had now remarried, while his father lived alone.

He had not enlightened her as to where his long, wide-nostrilled nose had come from, nor his grey eyes, his rounded chin and full yet sensitive mouth, probably because he had not bothered to delve into the history of his family's facial structure.

It was impossible to forget, too, the way his features, after they had loved and lain entwined, had come alive from their usual inscrutability. His possessive hold on her body, as if he were secretly afraid she would run away, showed her that, beneath his outward show of detachment and self-containment, he too had needs as profound as any man.

Her mother hugged her when she appeared for breakfast. 'Sorry we were so late home last night, darling,' Sybil Pemberton said.

'Good party, Mum?' Naomi took her seat and tackled with relish the food her mother placed in front of her.

'Well, it was a dinner party,' Sybil explained. 'We enjoyed it, but you would have been bored to death. Four gossiping middle-aged couples—just imagine!'

Naomi laughed. As she ate, finishing with coffee, there was a lengthy silence from her mother. She was washing the breakfast dishes and gazed minutely at each piece of crockery. Naomi knew her mother's eyes were not seeing them. In fact, she knew exactly what was coming next. It was always the same question.

'How's that dear little baby?'

Naomi replaced her empty cup. 'Becky? She's fine, Mum, she's really beautiful. Just like Clare. Mum——' she rose and put her hands on her mother's shoulders, 'won't you let me bring her here?'

Sybil's head shook slowly. 'Your father would blow his top. You know how disgusted he is with the whole thing. He'd go into a tantrum again about the way Clare treated—well, everyone, everything.'

Naomi knew only too well about her father's indignation, plus his refusal to meet either the baby's father or to see the baby.

'Then come back with me today——'

Sybil put aside the tea towel and turned to her daughter. 'I couldn't do it, dear, then come home and say nothing to your father. I'd be bubbling over about Becky and want to talk to him. I just couldn't take his annoyance at my "disloyalty", as he'd call it, in going near Clare's little mistake.'

Naomi shrugged her elegantly sloping shoulders. Afterwards, they drooped disconsolately. 'What would have happened if I'd taken Dad's attitude? That poor baby . . . Brian . . . he wouldn't have been able to cope. Think of how it would have felt to have had your only grandchild taken into care!'

'Naomi, don't!' Sybil went across to her daughter who had resumed her seat, and rested her cheek against the silky, simply-styled hair. 'Don't think your dad and I don't appreciate the way you gave up your job to go and look after Becky. You always were the caring one, darling. You wouldn't ever have done what Clare did.'

Naomi shook her head fiercely. Sybil went to put away the dishes she had dried, while Naomi took her coffee cup and saucer to the sink to wash them. 'Mum,' she said after a while, 'Gareth phoned last night.'

'Naomi!' Sybil's eyes were bright. 'After saying he wouldn't, too! Couldn't he wait?' Her mother said the words with fond indulgence, not with the sharpness which she herself had used to Gareth.

'So he said. I was so surprised to hear from him, it kind of—well, threw me off balance. I wasn't very pleasant to him. Mum, there was so much I wanted to say——' If only she could have poured out her feelings to Gareth as she was to her mother now.

'He took it badly?' Again, Naomi nodded.

'We almost quarrelled. In the end, he just put the phone down on me.' Her mother was silent. 'I suppose I could write, say I'm sorry, tell him how much I——'

'Why don't you phone him now, dear?'

'You don't mean it?' Her mother nodded. 'Midweek, on a working day? But he'll probably be out at the site.'

'If he is, leave a message asking him to contact you here.'

'But I'll have to leave soon, get back to Becky and Brian.'

This fact had apparently not occurred to Sybil. She brightened and urged, 'Phone him, anyway, just in case he's working in the office this morning.'

Watching her mother go upstairs, Naomi approached the telephone with some trepidation. After the abrupt ending by Gareth of their conversation last night, she could not imagine what kind of reception he would give her this morning.

Listening to the ringing tone at the other end, she wished her nervousness would stop tying her inside into knots.

'Site office.' The young, bright voice that answered was brimming with confidence.

Naomi closed her eyes. Slim, she visualised, short-sleeved blouse, grubby jeans, soft shoes, broken nails, but a pretty face and winsome ways. Was this why Gareth had grown angry at the mention of her longing for him to kiss her and love her?

'Can I help you?' the voice prodded politely.

'Sorry. Yes, I hope so. My name's Naomi Pemberton. I'd like to speak to Gareth, Mr Gareth Gill, if he's there.'

'Dr Gill?' So, Naomi thought, he's got his Ph.D.—but he didn't let me know. 'Yes, he's here,' the young woman answered. 'Just a moment, I'll put him on to you.'

Naomi clutched the receiver. Well, in a few seconds she would be talking to him. What should she say?

Two or three minutes went by. He must be busy, she thought, knowing now that her first words to him would be of apology for disturbing him.

The receiver was lifted. 'Are you there?' the young woman queried. 'I'm sorry, but Dr Gill's just on his way out to the site.'

'But couldn't I have just a word?' she persisted,

cursing the fact that the girl could not possibly miss the note of desperation. There was another pause.

'Sorry,' came the answer, 'but he's told me to give you a message.' Naomi brightened. 'The message is, Thanks for phoning, but don't call me, I'll call you. He said you'd understand. Okay? Must go now. 'Bye.' The connection was cut.

Her mother appeared at the top of the stairs. 'Well, dear?' she asked.

Naomi shook her head, unable to answer. Then she conquered the threatening tears. 'He was there.' Her head lifted. 'But he wouldn't speak to me, Mum, he just wouldn't speak to me.' And, she thought, I know why. That girl was the reason. He's found someone else.

'Don't do that often,' said Brian, handing Naomi the baby as she entered the flat. 'I mean, leave me alone for the night with her,' he nodded at the untidily dressed bundle, 'without help.'

'Bad night?' Naomi sympathised.

'Bad? It was awful! She just wouldn't stop crying.'

'She missed a woman's touch, didn't you, my pet?' She kissed the baby's head.

'For Pete's sake, don't rub it in!' Brian rubbed his eyes and felt his stubble. Becky started crying, and her father gave her a pained look and made a dash for the bathroom. 'Late for work already.'

'You can't run away from the consequences of your actions all your life, Brian,' Naomi called, looking fondly at her niece.

Brian opened the bathroom door a fraction. 'Hey, was that a warning shot across my bows? Have your parents been getting at you to——'

'Nothing of the sort, Brian,' Naomi answered mildly. 'My mother would love to see Becky. Dad—I just don't know about him. He's very conventional.'

'You can say that again,' Brian answered feelingly. 'You should have heard the blast in my telephone ear the day he heard his elder daughter was expecting! Blamed me, he did, as if he didn't know that two's required to produce——'

'Anyway,' Naomi interrupted, 'what I meant was that I won't always be here, will I?'

'Must get on.' The bolt on the bathroom door was shot home.

Having fed, bathed and dressed the baby, Naomi tackled the untidiness all around her. If Brian could not manage even for an evening and part of a morning to take care of himself and his child, what would the future hold for him?

What, indeed, did it hold for her? She stared through the bay window of the upstairs flat, which was part of an ageing, neglected house and watched the traffic pass. Her immediate future would be fully occupied by caring for Clare's baby, not to mention her abandoned boy-friend.

Further ahead, life for her seemed bleak, offering no fulfilment of her love for Gareth. Unless—the thought took her breath away—unless she told him the truth?

If they married after the two years was over, he would be part of the family, wouldn't he? Which meant there would be no barrier to his being told the facts about Clare's baby. It also meant that the barrier which had sprung from nowhere to separate them would, in its turn, be broken down.

Going out of the flat, she ran down the stairs to the pay telephone in the hall. She would phone him again, insist on speaking to him, and tell him why it wasn't possible for her to get away to visit . . . The memory of the sarcastic and unfeeling brush-off he had given her earlier that day stilled her hand in mid-air.

CHAPTER TWO

BRIAN'S widowed mother delighted in her little granddaughter. She did not worry how much of an 'error' the baby had been. Having the contented bundle in her arms seemed, at that moment, to be all she could ask of life.

The still-slim woman with untutored hair and simple, unco-ordinated mode of dress had a warm, bright manner and a quick-thinking way of speaking which, Naomi had reflected on other occasions when she had met her, contrasted so strongly with her own mother's personality.

Her mother was warm, too, but possessed a more well-cared-for look, hair which bore the stamp of weekly sessions at the hairdresser's, jackets and skirts with tastefully matching colours, plus a thought process which was more profound than fast.

'I do think,' commented Mrs Westley, 'in fact I'm sure, I can see a likeness to you in her, Brian.'

'Can you?' Eagerly, Brian moved to sit on the arm of his mother's chair and searched his daughter's face. Naomi was so touched by the sight of the young man seeking for a look of himself among tiny features which were predominantly Clare's, she felt like crying. Then his eyes lifted, searching for Clare in her own face.

Smiling sympathetically, she shook her head. It's no use, she was telling him wordlessly, playing a game of 'let's pretend'. I'm not Clare and you know it. Nor will I go on for ever being Becky's substitute mother.

Mrs Westley insisted on taking over the feeding of her grandchild while Naomi joined Brian at the tea table. As she watched the baby in her grandmother's arms, tears rose at the back of Naomi's eyes at the thought that her own mother was denied the pleasure of even seeing Becky, let alone feeding her. If only her father would change his attitude, and if only Clare hadn't run away so precipitately from her responsibilities, in more ways than one . . .

'Pity your car's being serviced, Brian,' Mary Westley regretted as she watched her son holding the handle of the pram which contained the sleeping form of the baby. 'Then you and Naomi wouldn't need to cope with the steps and the escalators on the Underground.'

'We'll take out the carrying section from the frame, Mrs Westley,' Naomi tried to assure her, 'and then we'll carry her between us.'

'Sometimes,' Brian added thoughtlessly, 'people don't see we've got a baby suspended between us and push past us.'

Seeing Mrs Westley's frown creep back, Naomi explained hurriedly, 'Most of the time people do see us, of course. Then they smile at the baby.'

The hasty reassurance seemed to work and a few moments later they were down the short garden path and waving goodbye to the baby's smiling grandmother.

They had left it later than usual to make their way back to Brian's place. The rush hour was in its early stages and commuters were battling with each other for supremacy in the race for home.

Anyone on normal human business as she and Brian were, Naomi thought, trying to keep a hold on her panic, was looked upon by all these people as irritants, whose sole object was to act as obstacles in their race to get the great city off their backs and the comforts of home wrapped around them.

Someone in the frenetic rush was carrying a large

suitcase in each hand. Naomi saw the cases first. Before she could take avoiding action, the suitcase nearest to her swung diagonally across her right leg.

As she pitched forward the case straightened, leaving the hard ground exposed for her to fall on. With a cry she took the impact on her knees, hip and right hand. Instinctively, she had not released her grip on the baby's cot, holding it high, although it sloped at an alarming angle.

'The baby,' she cried from the ground, 'is she all right?'

Another, stronger, hand prised hers from the handle, which was gripped by yet another, freeing her from the need to hold it. A woman lingered, but on discovering the victim was still breathing, hurried on. The rest raced relentlessly by, taking their scant sympathy with them.

All except the man with the suitcases, she discovered on attempting to rise. Two hands grasped her waist, lifted her upright. 'Where's Becky? Where's Brian?' she mumbled, looking with appeal into the tall man's face.

'I'm sorry I knocked you down,' the stranger said.

The deep voice brought her out of her dazed state. Her eyes showed her an outline plan of the man's features before her brain filled in the substance of the personality plus the identity. It couldn't be, it just couldn't!

'Gareth?' she whispered, pushing tremblingly at her hair. 'Oh, Gareth, it's wonderful to see you!'

As he scanned her face, she smiled at him tremulously. He made a lightning inventory of her injuries, then his glance darted from her to Brian, dropping to inspect the child in the cot. His jaw grew rigid, clamping down on the anger which had quickened his breathing. He thrust her from him, bent to reclaim his suitcases and strode away. In a few seconds he was lost in the crowd.

Later, Naomi could hardly recall how she managed to reach Brian's flat. Her knees throbbed, her hand and hip, both of which had taken the brunt of her fall, ached badly. Inside herself, she hurt most of all. Gareth had seen her, condemned her and spurned her in the space of a few unreasoning moments.

When Brian had asked her the man's identity, since she seemed to know him, she had shaken her head. Back home, while she put the baby to bed, he asked her again.

'Didn't you hear me say his name?' she answered. When he shook his head, she told him, 'That was Gareth—Gareth Gill.'

It took a few moments for her words to make an impact. Brian frowned, then asked with disbelief, 'That wasn't your boy-friend?'

'Get it right,' she commented bitterly, lifting the baby to her shoulder and patting her back, 'ex-boy-friend, from the look of it.'

Still Brian seemed puzzled, then realisation dawned. 'You don't mean he thought——' his finger indicated himself, then Naomi and last of all, Becky.

Naomi nodded. 'Obviously. After all, he gave me two years, didn't he, two years to make up my mind whether I wanted to marry him, or alternatively, to get myself another boy-friend.' She stood up with the baby in her arms. 'Seems he's decided I've done just that. Got myself a child, too.'

Brian took the baby, holding her gently. 'By me.'

'You're only too right.' Naomi's lips were tight with an unspeakable pain.

'But haven't you told him?'

'It's all a great big secret, isn't it? Keep all Clare's misdeeds in the family.'

'And ruin your life after you've done so much for Becky and me? Look, Naomi, I don't really care if you tell——'

'She's not your sister, is she?' The moment she had spoken the sharp words she was full of remorse. As a wave of pain contorted Brian's pleasant features, she added hastily, 'What I really meant was, you haven't got a father like mine. I mean, I'm very fond of him, but he's stuck in the past. You know what I mean?'

'About marriage and woman's place and a ring on her finger before she gets together with a bloke and produces the next generation? Yes, I know what you mean.' There was an unusual touch of bitterness in Brian's voice. He went on, 'And would you believe it, I think I'm getting stuck in the past, too, like your dad. When he was young, women had some sense of responsibility, didn't they? They didn't give birth to a baby like Becky, then up and leave her for a—a——'

'Career?' Naomi helped him out gently.

'Not forgetting the other bloke. Can you imagine Clare without a man?'

Not in any circumstances, Naomi thought, but did not say so.

That evening, Naomi phoned her mother. First, she asked if her father was in. No, her mother told her, so Naomi let it all come pouring out—about the fall, the meeting with Gareth and, last of all, his dismissal of her.

'Did you hurt yourself?' her mother asked at once.

'Various parts of me are aching, but I'll recover,' was Naomi's philosophical answer. 'Mum,' she continued tentatively, 'if I told Gareth the truth, would Dad mind very much?'

'He'd make my life a misery, dear. Please, Naomi,' Mrs Pemberton answered with some urgency, 'keep it a secret. You did promise.'

'But isn't it just as bad,' Naomi pleaded, 'that *I* should be thought to be the one who had a baby outside marriage?'

'More than anything, dear, it's the way Clare left

her baby that your father objects to so much. You know that.'

Naomi realised she was getting nowhere and sighed, sympathised with her mother and rang off. Although, she thought, why I should constantly be handing out sympathy to others when I'm really the one who needs it, I don't know. After all, aren't I suffering from the result of moral misdemeanours I didn't even commit?

It was three days later when the telephone called Naomi away from the television film she was watching. Brian was out, doing a carpentry job for a friend's mother, he had explained. It was a way of bringing in some extra cash, he'd added. Naomi, who was only too aware of how sparsely the money Brian brought home each week covered the cost of the necessities of life, did not hesitate to nod her approval.

It had to be her mother, she thought, her listless hand reaching out. No one else knew the telephone number of Brian's flat. She discovered she was wrong.

'Naomi?' The voice was heartbreakingly familiar, but its briskness did not in itself invite familiarity. Instead, it touched Naomi's heart with frost.

'Yes, Gareth?' It hurt to throw his briskness back at him.

There was a faint pause as if he were reorientating his thoughts. 'I called you to find out whether you were recovering from your injuries.'

Naomi had to catch her breath so that he would not hear how her lungs were overworking. 'Everything is healing up nicely, thank you.' Except my heart, she longed to add.

Another prolonged pause had that heart thumping. Was he about to ring off? 'How did you get my—this number?' she asked hastily.

'I rang your mother, thinking you'd be there. The moment I'd dialled, I realised how unthinking I'd been. Naturally you would have left your parents' home.' Naomi just went on listening, guessing what might be coming. To her surprise, the silence was not broken by him, so she attacked acidly,

'To live with my boy-friend who's the father of my child?'

'Precisely.'

'Precisely nothing!' she hit out, her voice full of the tears which had so taken her by surprise. 'You just don't understand.'

'Explain to me.' There was a touch of the old Gareth in the invitation and it was nearly her undoing.

'Explain?' she whispered. 'Gareth, I can't.' Oh God, she thought, we're back to where we were when he called me a few weeks ago. He had hung up on her then. Would he do so now?

This time, the silence was bruising. She could feel his pent-up feelings coming at her. 'Then consider our association ended,' he grated. 'I have no desire to hear from you, see you or *touch* you again!'

In a purely defensive movement, she replaced the receiver before the same action from his end could inflict on her a shattering humiliation.

Brian was working in a corner of the large kitchen. His tools and the materials he used were everywhere and wood shavings were scattered around.

Naomi closed her eyes to the chaos, forgot to remember that food was cooked and eaten in that room and burst out,

'It's no good, Brian—I can't take it any longer!'

His head came up slowly, and she could see he was covering with a thin veneer his dread of what was coming. 'Can't take what, Naomi?'

'Gareth's attitude to me. Brian, I must see him!'

'You mean one evening?' He resumed his work. 'Sure. Invite him here whenever you want.' His head receded more into his shoulders as if he was taking cover from what he guessed might be coming.

'What I want, Brian, is to go and see him.' The fair hair brushed his shirt as his head disappeared even more between his shoulders. 'Tomorrow's Friday, isn't it?'

The able fingers worked away without pause. 'You mean spend Friday night at your boy-friend's, then come home Saturday?'

Naomi frowned. Had she never told Brian where Gareth lived in the university vacation? Didn't he realise she couldn't go and stay at Gareth's father's place, just like that? 'No,' she persisted gently, 'I meant to go to my parents' house for the weekend. Returning Monday, of course.'

The head emerged from lowered shoulders. 'You mean—leave me alone with Becky for *three* nights? Have a heart, Naomi! A few hours coping with her's about as much as I can manage. Three nights!' He made an elaborate gesture of mopping his brow.

Slowly, Naomi approached the despondent figure. She watched the long-fingered hands, roughened from constant and heavy use, lie limply beside the two pieces of wood he had been dovetailing into an immaculate angle, and her own hand lifted to rest on his shoulder, drooping now.

'One day, Brian,' she said, 'you'll have to cope all the time.'

He tried to shake her hand—and the warning—from its hold. It would not move. His head turned and he took in the crumpled blouse, the creased skirt which did not hide her feminine attractions. 'I'll have to get myself another woman, then, won't I?'

Naomi reclaimed her hand, her heart sinking at the look in Brian's eyes. 'It's no good,' she told him quietly, 'you must get it into your head that I'm not Clare, even though we resemble each other so closely.'

'I wouldn't want you to be Clare, Naomi. You're made of better stuff than she is. You've got loyalty and love and——'

'Thanks, Brian,' she interrupted, 'but I'm going to see Gareth. Tomorrow evening, when you get home from work, I'll go to Sussex.'

'Thanks, Naomi,' he shot at her as she stood at the half-opened door, 'thanks a lot! Thanks for going off and leaving me, just to see a boy-friend who doesn't want you——'

'Is that all you've got to say to me after all I've done for you and Becky?' she choked, more upset by his comment about Gareth than his bitterness about her leaving him to cope alone.

The baby, in her small bedroom, started crying.

Brian rose at once, dusted his hands, wiping them on his woodworking apron. 'Sorry,' he answered, 'sorry, sorry. Didn't mean it . . .'

Naomi peered carefully through the open door of the baby's room. Brian had picked Becky up and was cradling her. Unaware that he was being observed he rubbed his cheek against his daughter's soft, dark brown hair.

Creeping away, Naomi had to swallow the lump in her throat. Making for her own room, she slumped on to the bed. This was all Clare's doing, she thought helplessly. How would it all end?

'I've left the baby's feeds until part-way through tomorrow,' Naomi told Brian as she stood at the living-room door, suitcase in hand.

It was early on Friday evening and Brian sat on the low couch reading a magazine. 'Thanks,' was his short answer. He did not lift his head.

Irritation grew in Naomi, sharpening her tone. 'Remember to keep everything clean, won't you?' She received a nod this time. 'And to warm the bottle containing the milk before you give it to Becky.'

'I have done it before, haven't I?' His head swivelled, his tone was annoyed, but Naomi forgave him because of the bleak look he gave her.

'Glad you haven't forgotten,' she countered. ''Bye till Monday, then.'

His hand lifted. It was the way it fell helplessly back to rest on the cushions that made Naomi give a silent sigh of despair.

Her father opened the door to her. He was a tall man, shoulders developing a slight stoop, his white hair thinning. She saw something of herself in him but, like Clare, she owed most of her looks to her mother.

Her father seemed surprised to see her as he bent to kiss her cheek and invite her in.

'I did phone,' Naomi remarked, on the defensive as she often was with him.

'Naomi darling!' Her mother, from the door of the living-room, held open her arms. Naomi hurried into them, dropping her case at her feet. Even at twenty-one, she found it good to feel her mother's arms around her. It was a much-needed reassurance in a rough, stressful world.

It told her also that she was doing right in looking after her baby niece in the absence of the child's real mother, despite her father's disapproval of the entire situation. Strangely, his attitude made her feel guilty, too, which was a feeling she did not like at all.

Later, when she had unpacked and had a meal, she sat with her parents in their living-room. The furniture was comfortable, the patterned loose covers hiding the worn parts. The carpet was of more recent origin, its turquoise colour highlighting one of the shades in the covered three-piece suite.

'Have you—have you seen anything of Gareth,

Mum?' Naomi had lowered her voice, hoping her father would not hear the question under the sound of the classical music playing in the background. Since his eyes did not move from their perusal of the evening's newspapers, she concluded that he had not heard.

'I saw him in the town, dear,' her mother answered, 'shopping with his father.'

'He hasn't called here to see you?'

Her mother smiled in a kindly way at the trace of hope in her daughter's eyes. 'He rang us to ask your telephone number in London.'

Naomi nodded. 'He wanted to know if I was recovering from hurting myself that day he tripped me up with his suitcases.' Her mother looked at her quickly, having noted the touch of acid in her daughter's tone. 'It wasn't because he wanted to make contact with me. In fact,' Naomi found she needed a deep breath to help her continue, 'he told me to consider our—our friendship at an end. He said he never wanted to hear from me again.'

Her voice had wavered, she hadn't been able to stop it. Her mother inspected the stitches of the piece of embroidery she was working on, her father turned a page of the tabloid newspaper.

Impulsively, Naomi turned to him. 'Dad——' she waited until she had his reluctant attention, 'I want to explain to Gareth. I want to tell him.' Her father slapped the newspaper on to his knees. Naomi braved his rising irritation. 'He saw me with Brian and the baby. He thinks the baby's mine and that Brian's the father!'

'If the man's fool enough to think that, then you're well rid of him.'

'How can you be so stupid, Father!'

The paternal rebuke in her father's eyes, plus her mother's exclamation of dismay, forced from her an immediate apology, but she followed this with the sourly-spoken statement, 'In law, it used to be called something like circumstantial evidence.'

Her father appeared unmoved. He retrieved the paper and began to read it. A glance at her mother told Naomi nothing. She picked up a paperback from its place on the arm of the chair, read through the introduction on the back and decided that it looked interesting.

For the remainder of the evening, it kept her occupied. It had, she concluded, as she closed its pages just before going to bed, acted as a kind of escape from her life's entanglements. Most of all, the developing story had pushed all thoughts of Gareth to the perimeter of her mind. Beyond that, she could not move him.

At breakfast next day, she told her mother that she intended to visit Gareth and his father. 'Just as you wish, dear,' her mother answered in a carefully neutral voice. 'His father still lives in the same house. I did hear he hadn't been too well lately. You know, a bit chesty—bronchial trouble. Left over from the years he used to smoke, I imagine.'

'Does Gareth live there all the time?' Naomi enquired. 'Since he came back south from York, I mean.'

'Now that I wouldn't know,' her mother answered. 'It's the long vacation, isn't it? Which means he wouldn't be needed at the university yet.'

Naomi nodded, remembering in detail the apartment Gareth had rented when she used to visit him in the past. She had been dazzled by him—his good looks, the driving determination in his eyes, eyes which could change at the snap of the fingers from the remote to the personal, then the intimate level.

He had been a lecturer with a formidable reputation and a string of academic qualifications, she a departmental secretary. When he had brought her work to do, she had carried it out with meticulous care in order to earn his praise.

Her desire to please him had increased as the months had passed, so that he would bring her more work, maybe to linger, leaning over her shoulder to explain technicalities. It became plain that he returned her interest the day he did just that—remaining beside her as she typed, resting his hand on her shoulder and playing with strands of her hair.

His touch had so disturbed her she had stopped working and lifted her head to gaze upward into his eyes. They were smiling and his lips were moving, forming words which had stopped her breath on an intake as he had asked if she might be free to go for a drink with him that evening.

It was not far to Gareth's father's house. She knew it well, remembering it from the past. A fit of coughing growing nearer told her in advance who would be answering her ring on the door bell.

'Naomi? Naomi Pemberton?' the man with stooping shoulders asked. He moved his thickening form backwards and with a wide-sweeping gesture, invited her in. 'It's good to see you again, Naomi.' He wore the jacket of a suit, shiny now with use and trousers which did not match. On his feet were almost-threadbare slippers, but his near-white hair had been cared for and cut neatly to within an inch or two of his shoulders.

A movement of his head invited her to join him in the front room. This again she remembered, but it had been allowed to deteriorate just a little as its owner's health had done. Another gesture indicated that she should sit down.

Naomi found a seat on the three-seater couch and she glanced over it nostalgically. Her subconscious, she realised, must have led her there, recalling the times she had lain on it with Gareth, making caressing love. Now, she found her eyes darting to the heavy oak door, but it remained partly open, just as her host had pushed it.

'He's upstairs, dear,' Eddie Gill told her, interpreting the reason for her eyes' hopeful movements. 'I expect you called to see him, didn't you?'

A bout of coughing almost drowned her answering 'yes'. A hand waved her through the door as the man lay back against the chair, endeavouring to recover.

Having closed the door behind her, Naomi climbed the stairs, her heart thumping more loudly than her footsteps. She remembered Gareth's bedroom, too. It held memories so sweet that even his dismissal of her could not erase them.

As she lifted her hand to knock, she saw that it was shaking. It had not even made contact with the wood when the door was opened, as if the man inside the room had sensed she was there.

There was a clash somewhere in her head, but she knew there was no real sound. Eyes meeting eyes made no noise. She tried to read the grey gaze that was regarding her, but it told her less than the set of his mouth and the hardened ridge of his cheekbones.

One thing she knew, his look contained no welcome, not even the gruff pleasure contained in his father's greeting. His son plainly felt no pleasure at all at the appearance at his door of the girl to whom he had given two years in which to make up her mind whether he was the right man for her.

You're still the man I want, she longed to cry out to him. Instead, she asked with stiff politeness, 'May I come in?'

'Why not?' he answered expressionlessly, moving back a few paces. Closing the door behind her, she faced him boldly.

Those cool grey eyes looked her over in a kind of

voyage of rediscovery. With a mute appeal which he chose to disregard, she tolerated the way his brooding gaze made an expert sketch of her still-rounded face, her arched brows and impudent nose. Her lips curved uncertainly as his gaze rested on them, passing over her smile and on to her neat chin.

The rest of her was examined with eyes half covered by drooping lids, only to lift again to her face as if he knew all he needed to know about the size and shape of her.

'So you couldn't wait those two years until I returned?'

His words almost knocked her backwards. Anger flared red in her cheeks. 'You're talking about the baby, of course.'

'Plus the devoted father. How long ago did you have his child?'

And I had intended, she thought, to tell this man the truth! 'If you mean how old is the baby, she's four and a half months.'

Insolent eyes skimmed her figure. 'You've recovered your shape remarkably well.' His lingering look made her flesh tingle and the essence of her throb with desire. It was a desire which, through its strength, overrode her fury. 'But, as I recall, you always were a champion of breast feeding.'

A vivid picture sprang into her mind of herself nursing a baby—*his* baby—giving to it through herself a flowing life force and a deep contentment such as he had once given her . . .

Her mind and body united in a desperate cry. *Even if you don't love me, I still love you.* Not a word of it was spoken.

Instead, she responded to his statement. 'I haven't changed my mind about that. But I have changed my mind about you. I know you didn't want to see me any more. You told me so on the telephone. All the same, I wanted to see you. Now,' she reached for the door handle and backed slowly out of the room, 'I don't care if we never meet again in the whole of our lives!'

A grasp of fingers swung her round, pulling her back. A violent foot kicked the door shut. 'But I do.' A movement jerked her against him. Her head went back and she stared into lawless eyes. 'Since I saw you last, you've become a woman. And no wonder!' His palm skimmed her breasts, briefly cupping one. Where he had touched her leapt to life. 'I want a taste of you again. Like this.'

Rigid fingers clamped on to the back of her head, while a barbarous mouth ground against hers, forcing it open. Teeth grated against teeth and his lips searched around the inner part of her mouth until she allowed him entry.

Her hands clamped for security on to his broad shoulders and she felt again the hard leanness of hips and thighs. An ice-flow within her began to melt under the lick of fire which seared its way through wherever her body made contact with his.

When he let her go, she had to struggle to catch her breath. Her cheeks seemed cold under the flatness of her shaking palms. His hands slid under the waistband of his worn denims and his ribs expanded and contracted as he, too, responded to the harder working of his lungs.

Their gazes locked and held, Gareth's containing a blaze which could have been cold fury or naked desire. Naomi fought vainly to discover which. Hers threw back at him defiance and unerring courage.

Starting to speak, she halted with dismay as the words were caught up in the thickness in her throat. Clearing it, she declared, 'I hope the taste of me you've just taken poisons you!' It was impossible to say more, since she knew her voice would waver and let him know just how much she really cared.

His father was nowhere to be seen as she ran from the house.

Brian's beaming smile greeted her from his workbench in a corner of the kitchen.

Naomi looked around, frowning. The whole place was so tidy, she could hardly believe her eyes.

'I've been a good boy, haven't I?'

Naomi could not restrain an answering smile at his goodnatured demand for praise. The fridge revealed that every bottle of feed she had left had been used. To her complete astonishment, she noted that they had also been refilled.

'Did you sterilise them all?'

'I did everything you told me to do, ma'am,' he replied, tugging at a non-existent forelock.

'And more, from the look of the kitchen.' She bent to inspect the floor, noted its complete lack of dust and rose. 'What came over you?'

'You came over me,' he joked. 'I couldn't bear to be told off by the beautiful substitute mother of my child.'

Naomi's hands went to her hips. 'You've played that bit of tape so often, Brian, it's getting worn. Now tell me the truth.'

'Hard-hearted woman, aren't you?'

'If I were, I wouldn't be here.'

Brian winced as her verbal missile hit the target. 'Okay, I'll give myself a dose of the truth drug. My mum stayed for the weekend—said she couldn't stand the thought of her beautiful grandchild being left to the tender mercies of its father.' There was a series of demanding cries from upstairs. 'There you are,' Brian pointed upwards, 'she's calling out for her granny to come and see to her.'

'Her granny'—but my mother's her 'granny' too.

The thought slipped in and out of her mind, leaving a tiny dart of pain in its wake.

Naomi glanced at her watch. 'Hey,' she said, 'what are you doing at home? It's Monday morning, remember? Or has your boss fired you for incompetence?'

'Incompetence?' Brian was wholly serious now. 'No one will ever fire *me* for that. I'm a damned good carpenter.'

He was right, and Naomi knew it. She also remembered too late how sensitive he was on the subject. 'Sorry, I was only joking.'

'If you must know,' Brian told her, only partly mollified, 'I told Tom, my boss, I wanted to finish this telephone table I'm making for the mother of one of my friends, so he gave me a couple of hours off.' His grin came back. 'He had to. He didn't want to lose his best worker, did he?'

Naomi laughed at Brian's boasting manner, but she was aware that it hid the multitude of uncertainties and self-doubts from which many creative people seemed to suffer.

It was after she had attended to the baby's needs, placing her in the carrycot on its folding stand beside an open window, that she went into Brian's bedroom to tidy it. The quilt had been straightened and everything was in its place. She sent a silent message of thanks to Brian's mother.

Her own room, which it was plain Mrs Westley had used, was as neat as she had expected. It was noticeable that even the dressing-table had been dusted. Looking away from her own mirror-reflection, thus avoiding the shadows beneath her brown eyes, she moved the bottle of her favourite perfume back into its customary place on the cosmetics tray.

That's curious, she mused, I didn't know Mrs Westley used perfume. The evidence was before her, however, and she gave a little smile as she concluded that every woman, regardless of age, liked to smell sweet. After all, didn't her own mother indulge herself occasionally by buying perfume from the neighbour who delivered a cosmetics catalogue through her door?

Becky was crowing at the coloured beads which were strung across the pram. Naomi lifted her out, changed her and lowered her to a rug which she had spread on the floor. The baby loved the unexpected freedom, kicking her legs and flailing her arms. When she flopped, Naomi turned her and tickled her middle, making the baby gurgle.

At last Naomi picked her up and cuddled her, feeling the young softness against her cheek and wishing with a vehemence which astonished even herself, I wish this baby were mine . . . *and Gareth's.* The last words came out of nowhere, freezing all her movements.

What was the use of thinking that way? she reproached herself. Everything there ever was between Gareth and herself was over. Why couldn't she accept the fact? Sighing, she replaced the baby in the carrycot. Her heart would break many times over before she could ever bring herself to do that.

CHAPTER THREE

Now and then, Brian received a letter or two requiring answers, and long ago he had prevailed upon Naomi to uncover her portable electric typewriter and answer the letters for him.

It kept her fingers supple, she argued with her better judgment, and helped her maintain her typing speed. But Brian's getting you to do more and more for him, her other side rebelled. When you do finally go, he'll miss your help so much he'll need to employ someone to clean, to type for him and, most important of all, to take charge of Becky.

The knowledge that Brian would never be able to afford to pay anyone to do those things filled her with a sense of utter hopelessness. It was a feeling with which she was growing painfully familiar. Interwoven into it all was the persistent longing to break away, to run to Gareth and tell him everything.

Then, she told herself, he would open his arms and she would rush into them, and all her problems would be solved. Coming out of her dream, she forced herself to start her next housewifely task, and the next, plus the next after that . . .

Naomi hurried away after paying the milkman at the front door. The baby was crying and Naomi, concluding that a back-patting session was called for, lifted Becky out of the cot, tapping her gently.

When the baby was cooing contentedly, she put her carefully on to her front again, watched her making a determined attempt to lift herself by pressing down on her hands, then turned her on to her back.

As she let her fingers walk gently upwards to the

tiny chin, her laughter mingled with the baby's chuckles. Kneeling, she bent to bury her face in the baby-softness, then moved to rest on her hands. Studying the fair skin of the little face, the soft hair which was as brown as her own, she could see both her sister and herself in the tiny features.

I wish you were mine—and Gareth's.

'I never thought you had it in you to love a child of yours so much.' The caustically-spoken words came at her from the door, taking away her high colour and bringing her to her feet. Thank God, she thought, her own words had not been spoken!

'I'm not a ghost.' Gareth strolled towards her. 'I don't walk through doors. It wasn't locked, so I pushed. Do you usually leave your doors unbarred for the benefit of all comers?'

There was, she knew, an insult implicit in the question, but she chose to disregard it. 'How did you know where I lived?'

'Your mother told me.' He looked around the furnished room, at the heavy mirror over the Victorian fireplace, up at the high, decorated ceiling, dull with dust collected over the years. 'Rented accommodation?' Naomi nodded. 'Do you work as well as take care of your child?'

Becky's not my child. Once again the words stayed in her head.

'With a baby as young as this, it just wouldn't be possible, would it?' she answered levelly, holding her head proudly.

'I imagine with a grandmother as your mother surely is, it shouldn't be difficult. You could live at home then, and carry on with your secretarial job at the university.'

'Thanks for your neat and tidy suggestions for the arrangement of my life, but I repeat, it just wouldn't be possible.'

Gareth seemed puzzled, looked round the room again. He must have seen Brian's brown, worn sweater slung across a chairback, waiting for Naomi to darn the holes in the sleeves.

Understanding dawned, and his expression grew unpleasant. 'So you live with the baby's father?'

If she told him the truth, she knew all the wrong conclusions he would draw. Nevertheless, she replied, 'I live here. The baby's father lives here. Make what you like of that.'

A flash like a controlled explosion flared briefly in his eyes. 'I should have worked that out from the start.' Again he looked her over, making Naomi wish her close-fitting top was not so revealing of her shape. 'I take it he's the one who brings in the money?'

'You take it right,' she flung back acidly, hating the censure in his eyes. 'He's a carpenter, a darned good one, but his pay is hardly a fortune, so he makes it up by doing evening work for friends and contacts. We have enough to live on—just.'

'You look tired.'

His switch from the general to the personal rocked her mentally, but she forced her face to stay blank. 'Being a housewife's no picnic, especially with no washing machine. Our secondhand one broke down. It's too old to mend.'

'House*wife*?' His tone told her of his contempt. He chose to ignore the rest of the information. He lifted her left hand, saw no wedding ring and dropped it. 'Wouldn't house-*woman* be more accurate?'

Naomi pressed her lips together in case they hurled the truth at him, taking the sneer from his expressive mouth and putting admiration for her courage into his eyes. 'Why did you come here, apart from wanting to insult me?'

'To see where you live, the kind of conditions your boy-friend's keeping you in.'

'You really do like to kick a girl when she's down, don't you?' she attacked, her mouth growing dry with anger. 'I've discovered something about you I didn't know. You're a cold-hearted swine, Gareth Gill. I don't like you any more.'

His face grew pale and she knew it was with suppressed fury, not sadness. 'Nor even want me?'

Yes, she wanted him, the whole daunting length and breadth of him. She wanted the pressure of his mouth against hers again, the possessive hold of his hands on her body. She would have given anything, almost, to see once more, just once, the love his look had held that evening he had made love to her and taken her to him, making them one.

His eyes flickered as they watched her changing expression, and she was forced to witness his small smile of victory as he guessed her thoughts. As he turned to the door, Becky gurgled. He looked down at her, then at Naomi.

'I've never seen such an incredible likeness.'

'It's the family look,' she answered desperately. 'She's got my mother in her, and—and Clare.'

'Not to mention,' he took her up scathingly, 'her father's eyes and his mother's nose.' He came closer, lifting a hand and pinching her chin, forcing up her face. 'Just what are you trying to tell me?'

He waited a moment, giving her time to answer, but she had been sworn to secrecy. Gareth discarded her chin and reached the door, turning once to look at her again. 'Just fade from my life, will you,' he said savagely, 'just fade. Leave me alone. That's all I ask.'

Naomi couldn't answer, her throat was too thick with emotion. Her head moved hopelessly from side to side, her teeth maltreated her bottom lip. He was going, and there was nothing she could do about it. His footsteps rang on the thinly-carpeted stairs. Was there really no way she could stop him?

There was a way! Her feet moved of their own free will, taking her on to the landing. 'Gareth,' she cried, 'wait a moment!' He turned, his brows lifting indifferently. 'There's something I want to tell you. Will you come upstairs again?' He did not move. 'A few minutes, only a few minutes?'

Her power over him, it seemed, had not quite disappeared. He climbed up the stairs, two at a time.

Becky was back in the carrycot, making baby noises. Soon it would be time for her morning's sleep. Beneath her agitation, Naomi was aware of the fact.

'I suppose you're going to tell me the child's not yours? That it's your sister's? After all, she has a look of her, as well as you, about her.'

Naomi's eyes came alive with hope. Had he known all along? She had missed completely the taunt in his words.

'That's right—it's Clare's. Her baby and Brian's.'

'Mm, that's what I thought you'd say.' It was unmistakable now, that irony.

Naomi frowned, her excited heartbeat slowing. 'But it's true, Gareth, it's true!'

'Is it?' His upraised brows and empty gaze told her how unconvinced he remained. 'A classic answer to a classic situation. Girl finds she's pregnant, gets desperate after baby's born so tells the world it's not her own little mistake, but that of her absent sister.' He pushed his hands into his cord slacks pockets. 'Okay, I'll buy it, since you obviously expect me to. Is that all you called me back to tell me? You're not going on to say that now that little matter is cleared up,' he nodded towards the carrycot, 'our relationship is back to where it left off and that I can marry you with impunity?'

'Is that what you think?' Naomi was speaking hoarsely, a hand to her throat. 'That I'd trick you into marrying me?' The baby's noises grew louder. 'If you even so much as ask me, Gareth, I'd throw your proposal right back in your face!'

Becky was crying now, the raised voices seeming even to have affected her adversely. Naomi raced across the room and picked up the baby, comforting her, turning to face her tormentor with a brave defiance.

'Your statement that Clare is the mother,' Gareth challenged, 'substantiate it.'

'I can't—you know I can't.'

'Where did the birth take place, for instance? Which hospital would have the records?'

Naomi stared at him, having no answer. Clare had disappeared out of the family's sight for the months leading up to the baby's birth. When she had returned in a taxi with the rolled up bundle in her arms, no questions were asked. Even Brian, Naomi discovered, had not been told where Clare had gone, nor where she had come from.

Gareth half rested against an armchair back. 'Would your mother or your father tell me where *Clare* gave birth to her child?' The emphasis on Clare's name told of his continuing disbelief.

Naomi shook her head. 'It was hushed up, the pregnancy, the birth, everything. It's still a family secret. I wasn't even allowed to tell you. I kept asking my mother if I could, but she said my father wouldn't forgive her for letting me tell anybody, even you, nor would he forgive me. So I've broken the family's ruling. Will you please keep the information entirely to yourself?'

There was no reply to her question.

'Please, Gareth?' He was even forcing her to beg him to stay silent! 'Can I trust you not to?'

He straightened with a jerk. 'You can trust me—as I trusted you. I may or may not let you down—as you let me down. And I don't care a damn whether you spend sleepless nights wondering exactly what my intentions in the matter are.'

At the door he threw at her, 'This time, don't call me back just to pour lying trivialities in my ear!'

As she heard the front door slam, Naomi found that Becky had fallen deeply asleep with her head nestled against her shoulder. When she was lowered gently on her side into the high-railed cot, her small white jacket was damp with tears, but she never even knew.

Naomi had baked all day—cheese straws, biscuits, vol-au-vents. She had made fillings and spooned them in, cooking where necessary. It was all intended for Brian's bring-a-bottle party.

In between baking, Naomi had waited hand and foot on Becky, who was beginning to learn the power of her cry. Naomi did not begrudge the work that had been forced on her. She accepted without question the fact that it had been Brian's turn to entertain his friends, having been entertained so often by them at their parties. He had little enough social life, she reflected as she worked, since he spent most evenings bent over his workbench.

The practical parts, such as using the saw, he carried out in the messy back yard which had once been a small Victorian garden. During the day, his work bench was covered, his tools put away for safety.

Having given Becky her final feed, she placed her in the carrycot, putting it on to the back seat of Brian's ageing car and securing it with the straps which Brian had fixed for that purpose. Mrs Westley had willingly agreed to have Becky for the night.

Driving through the slow-moving traffic, Naomi made her way along the packed streets to the little house in which Brian's mother lived. Age-wise, it was of approximately the same vintage as that in which

Brian rented his flat. It was, however, better furnished and better cared for.

'Are there many coming?' Mrs Westley asked, lifting her granddaughter into her arms.

Naomi lifted her shoulders. 'All those Brian's invited, plus others who weren't.'

'I wish you joy,' said Mrs Westley at the front door as Naomi prepared to leave. 'Sooner you than me, dear.' Still holding Becky, she rested a hand on Naomi's arm. 'I'll say it again, Naomi—I'll never be able to thank you enough for giving up your job and for all you're doing for Brian and Becky.'

Naomi squeezed the older woman's hand. 'Don't worry about it. Whatever I did, and am doing, I've done it with my eyes open. My sister Clare behaved so badly . . . Besides,' she kissed a fidgeting Becky's cheek, 'I love my sister's baby.'

Waving as she drove away, Naomi's smile faded. She thought unhappily, If only it had been just my job I gave up . . .

Brian was home by the time Naomi returned. He had stuffed a canapé into his mouth and held another. Naomi pounced on him, horrified.

'You can't gobble up all those! It's taken me hours, in between looking after Becky, to make the things!'

Brian's eyes glistened as he looked at the array of delicacies. 'Who did you think you were catering for, a gathering of your sophisticated friends? My mates'll make short work of those, then look round for more, like——'

'Bags of potato crisps?' Naomi opened a box and showed Brian the packets of 'ready salted' and 'flavoured' inside. 'Peanuts, cheese rolls?' She removed the lid of a large polythene box and he peered in. 'Okay for your mates?' she asked with a broad smile.

Brian grinned back, dusting his hands after

swallowing the second petite but tasty savoury. 'How did you guess my friends had big mouths?'

'And big appetites to go with them. Well, I hope there's enough there to keep them happy. If not, they'll just have to go hungry, won't they?' She opened a cupboard and saw cans piled high. 'Hey, how many are coming to this party? You've bought far too much beer, especially as they're bringing a bottle each.'

'If there's any over—and there won't be—I can drink it whenever I feel thirsty, can't I?'

'You sound as if you're intending to become an alcoholic,' Naomi joked.

Brian stared at her, his lower lip pushed out. 'There are times,' he answered, 'when I feel like taking to drink. Especially when I look at you.' He took a step nearer.

Naomi automatically backed away. 'You see Clare, not me.'

His gaze was intense. He was shaking his head. 'I can see you.'

'Sorry, Brian,' Naomi spoke as briskly as her apprehension would allow, 'there's nothing I can do about my similarity to Clare. I'm doing all I can to make up for her shortcomings by looking after her—and your—child. Don't get the wrong idea and expect anything more of me. You should know by now, I'm not made like that.'

The ringing of the telephone cut across the strange tension. 'That's probably one of your friends asking about the party.' Naomi gestured to Brian to answer it.

He had turned sulky. He lifted the receiver and said, 'Yeah?' He listened. 'Who? Oh—oh, yes, this is her boy-friend speaking. Yeah, she's here, beside me.' He held the receiver a short distance away. 'You want to speak to a guy called Gill, Gareth Gill?' He did not wait for her response. 'Sorry,' he said into the mouthpiece, 'she wants to have nothing more to do with you.'

Naomi went white, wrestled for possession of the receiver and won. 'Gareth? I'm sorry, Gareth. Everything Brian said was untrue. He's—he's just got a chip on his shoulder.'

'Is that so?' he answered, his voice dripping with sarcasm. 'He didn't sound to me like a man with a grudge. After all, he's got you, not to mention the child you and he produced together. What more could a man want?'

Exasperated, she replied, 'He hasn't got me. Becky is not my baby.'

There was a pause, then he said, 'Isn't it time you married your daughter's father?'

'I've told you the truth about that.' Gareth made no response, so Naomi finished, 'I must go. There's a party here tonight.'

Naomi replaced the receiver quietly, but her arm was shaking. She was glad Brian was out of the room. It gave her a chance to recover her composure.

The party was halfway through, yet still there were fresh faces filling the doorway. Food was circulating, like the drink. Fortunately, some guests had brought sandwiches and cakes to add to the food which Naomi had provided.

Brian was lying back on an armchair with a girl half-reclining on top of him. She was dark-haired, her eyes were brown, and he was gazing into them. Naomi had sunk, exhausted, on to the settee. For a few moments she was its sole occupant, but her blissful solitude did not last. A young man slumped beside her.

'Hi, gal,' a familiar voice addressed her.

Naomi's head shot round. 'How did you get here?'

Brian gazed at her, smiling stupidly. 'Where's the girl you were kissing just now?'

'I got rid of her, didn't I? You were sitting here all alone. I wasn't going to let you go to waste, was I?' His words were slurring into each other.

'You've had too much to drink, Brian. I warned you——'

'And I warned you, didn't I?' His eyes fixed on her brown gaze. I remember, Naomi recalled, that this was just the way he had been looking at that other girl. 'You're Clare,' his voice had lowered, 'that's who you are.' His hands fixed on to her shoulders.

Naomi was shaking her head frenziedly when someone shouted, 'Break it up, Brian! Some more of your mates have arrived.'

Brian glanced over his shoulder, brought his head back, then immediately turned round again. Naomi followed his eyes. While the newcomers had elbowed and kneed their way in, one lone male stood out from the crowd. He, it seemed, had no intention of joining the mêlée.

The lights had been lowered and the man lingered in the shadows. He leaned sideways against the doorway, hands in the pockets of his tan zipped jacket. His casual slacks fitted smoothly over his lean hips and thighs, while the brown polo-necked sweater he wore followed the line of his broad chest.

Naomi paled under his shrivelling scrutiny. 'It's Gareth, Brian,' she said, her throat dry, 'let me go over to him.'

Brian's hold on her shoulders did not loosen. 'You're my girl, not his,' he slurred. 'You're staying right here—here in my arms,' they went round her, 'and I'll never let you go.'

Naomi began to fight him, pushing at his shoulders, but even in his stupor his determination to hold on to her did not weaken. His beer-dampened mouth lowered on to hers and she squirmed under his first-ever kiss.

Something, someone, tugged his heavy weight from her shaken body.

'Who the——?' Brian spluttered, then recognised his adversary. 'What did you do that for?' he demanded, simulating bully tactics. 'She's my girl, my woman. She's Becky's mother——'

'You'll be sorry you said that, Brian.' Naomi was getting to her feet, pushing back her hair. She had not dared to meet Gareth's eyes.

'I'll be sorry, will I?' Brian answered thickly. 'What'll you do, walk out on me like——' He stopped abruptly, looked from her to Gareth and back.

'Finish your sentence, Brian,' Naomi urged, her voice pitched low and threatening. 'For my sake, finish the sentence. Or shall I finish it for you?'

He tossed his head back in disgust, made an unpleasant and disclaiming sound and slouched away.

Naomi turned to Gareth, her eyes wide with misgiving. 'He's not usually like that,' she attempted to explain, hoping to take the condemnation from the steely eyes that watched her implacably. 'He's had far too much to drink.' The noise of the beat music over the sound of raucously raised voices grated on the nervous system.

'Don't try to justify your lover's behaviour to me,' Gareth snapped.

Naomi shook her head, feeling as drunk from the jarring clash of sounds as Brian was from alcohol. 'Why did you come?' she asked.

There was a wave of movement behind her and she found herself pushed against Gareth. Her hands came up, resting defensively on his chest. He did not move with the crowd, but stayed like a statue rooted in cement.

In a matter of seconds, he had become her rock to which she could cling and turn to for stability in the almost intolerable charade of a life which she had taken upon herself to play out.

Her cheek sought for and found the haven of his chest and, for hours it seemed to her strained mind, she discovered again the deep contentment he had given her that night they had made love and said goodbye.

The contentment this time lasted no longer than that so-called love had endured then. Gareth forced her away from him by her shoulders. His hand slipped to her wrist and he tugged.

'Show me somewhere quiet,' he commanded.

He was pulling her towards the door. 'Why, why?' Her question went unanswered. She stared back over her shoulder, looking for Brian. He had a girl on his knee, the same dark-haired girl as before.

'Becky's room. She's with Brian's mother for the night.' Naomi indicated the small bedroom and he pulled her into it, switching on the light and pushing at the door. He did not let her go, but caught her other wrist, pulling her against him again. A throb started low down. She recognised it as desire and fought it madly. His eyes moved quickly over her features, coming to rest on her lips.

When she moved them, speaking to him, he watched their movement as if fascinated. 'I told you there was going to be a party here. You don't like parties. Well, you didn't when we—when we knew each other before. You don't like Brian, you don't like me, so why did you come?'

'No, I don't *like* you, you two-timing little bitch. But I can't keep away from you. In fact,' his eyes sparked cold fire, 'you draw me to you even more now than two years ago—if that's possible. I'm even willing to marry you, adopt the baby——'

'I don't want you to adopt her!' Naomi's voice rose with despair.

'Which shows,' he said through drawn-back lips, 'just how much you want to stay with the child's father.'

'No, no . . . you *must* understand, she's not mine to adopt.'

'Adopt?' The door was shouldered open. Brian sagged against the frame. 'Nobody's going to adopt my child. She belongs to me, me and——' His quick glance went to Naomi. 'Mine and hers. No one's going to take her away.' There was despair in his voice, too, catching at Naomi's compassion. He lurched into the room and grabbed the edges of Gareth's jacket.

Gareth did not raise a hand to stop him.

'You can't take *her* away, either,' a movement of Brian's head indicated Naomi. 'How would I look after Becky on my own?'

Gareth's expression was serious, but it bore no animosity. With something like pity, he removed himself from Brian's grip, who immediately sagged at the knees. At once Naomi went to him, giving him support as far as the door.

Outside, she called to one of his friends, who came and took him over, making encouraging noises. Naomi returned to the little bedroom and faced Gareth.

He was standing, hands in the back pockets of his trousers, features unreadable, waiting for her. His self-assurance so annoyed her, she walked over to him.

'I don't give that,' her two hands lifted and she clicked them in his face, 'for your offer of marriage. *Even willing to marry you.*' She threw back his words. 'How kind, how charitable of you to make me such a benevolent proposition!'

A wall of fire burned its way across his eyes. He gripped her arms and forced her body to collide with his. He ground himself against her so that she could feel his arousal.

The spreading heat of desire which she experienced at such a calculated intimacy as he was forcing on her brought her hands to his shoulders. Her breath came quickly as she gasped, 'Oh, God, Gareth . . . I love you!'

Her eyes searched for his, looking for that blaze of passion which they had held the evening they had become one in the first thrusting, possessive encounter. All she found was a furious, unnerving contempt. He broke free, just as he had pulled away from all contact with the drunkenly clinging Brian.

His lips twisted. 'Keep your love—and your lies—for your boy-friend and your child!'

He was out of the room and the house before she could think of a word in self-defence.

With the door to the room wide open, the party's side-effects intruded. They filled the baby's room with cigarette smoke and the pervasive smell of spilt alcohol from discarded empty containers.

It took all Naomi's courage and fighting spirit to assume the hostess-look of smiling indulgence, and move out again to mingle with Brian's guests. No one bothered to make way for her. Men and their girl-friends half-lay on the floor, their heads resting against the furniture, talking a kind of love-language which only they appeared to understand.

Other groups talked, some deadly serious, some rocking on their chairs with laughter. The food seemed to have run out long ago, but nobody cared, since the drink had outlasted it.

Brian was across the room, leaning forward, head on hand. He appeared to be at the maudlin stage of over-indulgence, clinging with a false affection to the girl who, earlier, had seemed only too happy to be lying across him.

Now, she seemed embarrassed, looking round for help. Naomi made her way towards them. 'Hi, Brian,' she said softly. He did not respond. Naomi asked the girl her name, then said to Brian, 'Let Jan's arm go. Come on,' she prised his fingers away and the girl escaped. 'Hold on to me, if you like,' she encouraged.

'Don't want you,' he mumbled. 'You're going to leave me and take my Becky away.'

'You're wrong,' Naomi answered gently. 'I wouldn't take your baby away from you. I don't have the right, do I?'

'No, you don't.' His head came up heavily. 'Yes, you do. She's yours as well as mine.'

'But, Brian, you know very well——'

'Get the hell out,' he muttered, hiding his face again.

Naomi mouthed to the friend who sat on the arm of Brian's chair, 'He's best in bed, Johnnie. Could you——?' She pointed along the hall.

The young man nodded, trying to pull his friend to his feet. Having made it, Brian sank back again. Johnnie tugged him up for the second time, called to someone to help him and together they eased Brian into a fireman's lift over Johnnie's shoulder. Brian did not murmur a word of objection.

Later, in the early hours, when the party was over, Naomi sat among the debris of hurled bread rolls, dented beer cans and bottles which had emptied themselves on to the carpet. Although the room was empty, the banter still shot back and forth between her ears, the beat of music still throbbed inside her head.

Standing out from the chaos in her mind was the fiery encounter with Gareth. She could not forget the anger of his leavetaking, nor the condemnation in his eyes.

Exhaustion made her sleep until noon. Horrified, she flung aside the bedclothes and raced to the bathroom to wash. Having dressed and eaten as much cereal and milk as she could force herself to swallow, she called Brian's mother on the phone.

'Don't worry,' Mrs Westley assured her. 'My granddaughter and I are doing fine, aren't we, love?' There was a coo from the baby, making Naomi laugh with relief.

'I was flat out,' she explained. 'I told myself to leave the mess until today, but once I started clearing up, I couldn't stop.'

'No wonder you slept late, then,' Mrs Westley soothed. 'Is Brian up yet? If not, his boss will be after him when he gets to work.'

Naomi frowned. 'There was no sign he'd had breakfast, so he must still be in bed. I'll go and wake him and get him fed, then I'll be round for Becky.'

'That'll be fine, dear. Tell Brian not to be too long, won't you? Only I think I've got one of my bad chests coming on and I don't want to give a cold or anything to the baby.'

'As soon as I can,' Naomi promised, and rang off.

Hurrying along to Brian's room, she opened the door. The bed was empty. The covers had been neatened and on the pillow there was a note.

'Sorry about this,' the note ran, 'but I've had a good job offer somewhere else. It's better pay than I've been getting.'

Naomi, feeling her cheeks drain, sank on to the bed. She read on, 'Sorry to let you down, Naomi, but I had to go. Look after Becky for me. I know you love her like I do. Sell my car and use the money, if you like. I've paid the rent until the end of the month.'

Naomi discovered that the paper was curling under the moistness of her fingertips. Brian's letter went relentlessly on. 'After that,' it said, 'I expect your mum and dad will have you and Becky, or if not, my mum will. Thanks a lot. I'll be in touch some time. Brian.'

CHAPTER FOUR

BRIAN'S mother had gone so pale, Naomi grew worried. The note was in her long, thin hands and the paper shook. Strange, Naomi thought, staring at her with compassion, how I haven't thought of her as being over sixty until now.

'Can I get you something, Mrs Westley?' she asked.

'Thanks, dear.' Even her voice had grown older. 'There's probably still a cup of tea in the pot from the quick one I had while I was waiting for you. Have one yourself,' she called as Naomi hurried into the kitchen.

Carrying in two cups of tea on a plastic tray she had found, Naomi lowered it to the unoccupied half of the couch. Gladly, Mrs Westley swallowed the hot drink while Naomi drank hers more slowly.

'Whatever got into him?' mused Mrs Westley, scanning the note again as if hoping that the order of the words had changed and Brian hadn't gone away after all. 'I've never brought him up to run away from his responsibilities.'

'What about Clare, Mrs Westley,' Naomi took her up, 'what about my own sister? Didn't she run away, too?'

'That poor little mite,' Brian's mother commented, looking across the room to where Becky lay kicking her legs and reaching out for the coloured beads. 'No mother, and now no father. But she's got her granny still. I won't desert her.'

'Nor me, Mrs Westley,' Naomi asserted. 'I know you're not fit enough to look after her, but I'll take her to my parents' house. My mother won't mind having the two of us living there, until—well, until Brian comes home.'

'Are you sure, dear?' There was hope now in Mrs Westley's eyes.

'Of course I'm sure.' Naomi crossed her fingers. She wished she were as sure of her father as she was of her mother. 'She is Becky's other granny, after all.'

'I'm so glad, Naomi.' Mrs Westley's hand reached out and Naomi held it tightly.

'You didn't really think I'd desert Becky, too? After all, she is my niece.'

'She looks so much like you, dear, anyone would think she was yours. I expect they do, don't they?' Naomi nodded. 'Do you mind? I mean, you not having a ring on your finger . . .'

'I don't mind, Mrs Westley.' But I do mind, she was thinking, I mind so much it nearly kills me. I'd never have a man's baby, then walk off and leave him like Clare did. I'd never behave as Gareth thinks I've behaved.

The thought of Gareth brought a pain of a different kind. She told herself to stop thinking about him. He had gone from her life, so what was the use of looking on him as part of it?

Mrs Westley was tearful as she kissed her granddaughter's pink cheek. Naomi piled Becky's clothes and covers into a large bag and, together with the carrycot's frame, put them into the car boot. Then she hugged Mrs Westley and carried Becky to the back seat of the car.

No sooner had she entered the flat and put the carrycot down than the telephone rang. Hoping it was Brian with an address at which she could contact him, she hurried to silence its ring.

'Naomi?' It was her mother's voice and it occurred to Naomi that her mother was speaking softly. 'Your father's away for the day, and I just thought—well, the idea came to me that——'

'You might come and see Becky?' Naomi could not hide her delight. 'Oh Mum, of course. And if Dad's out, why are you speaking so quietly?'

Her mother laughed. 'Sheer habit, I assure you. I hate keeping anything from him, but he's so stubborn about this, about Clare and everything, it goads him every time I so much as mention her name. Anyway,' she spoke more normally now, 'I'm all dressed and ready to catch the train. I'll drive to the station. Now, when I arrive in London, which Underground line do I take?'

Having given her mother the appropriate instructions, Naomi ran across to the baby, lifted her out and hugged her. 'Your other granny's coming to see you, Becky,' she informed a passive baby. 'I must have a bite to eat, give you your feed, then think of something for our evening meal.'

Becky gurgled as if she had understood every word. Laughing, Naomi dropped a blanket to the floor, then knelt and lowered Becky on to it. Two hours later, Naomi ran down to answer the door bell's ring. She welcomed her mother as if it had been years since they had met.

As they drew apart, Sybil Pemberton looked into her daughter's face. 'I know there's something wrong, love, don't try to deny it.' She followed Naomi up the wide staircase. 'Is it finally getting to you, looking after your little niece? I thought it might, you know. It was an awful responsibility for you to take on . . .'

Her voice had tailed off. For the first time, she had caught sight of her small granddaughter. Sybil Pemberton stared down at the sleeping baby. When Naomi saw the tears in her mother's eyes, she put her arm round her, but knew nothing would ease the awful pain nor affect the exquisite pleasure her mother must now be feeling.

'She's the image of Clare,' Sybil whispered.

'Most people say how like me she is.'

Sybil shook her head. 'A faint resemblance, maybe, but she's Clare all over.' She smiled at her younger daughter, but Naomi knew she was not really seeing her. 'I'm Clare's mother, they're not. I know the exact difference between you, and,' her eyes swung to Becky again, 'it's Clare I see there, not you. Not really.'

Sybil seemed to need to sit down. Naomi led her to the couch and sat beside her. 'Oh, Clare,' her mother was whispering, 'how could you do what you did?'

Naomi made no attempt to reply. She was not Clare, her mother had made that clear. There was no comfort she could offer to this saddened lady who was her mother, yet who, in a matter of moments, had become something of a stranger. And yet she herself needed her mother so much at that moment . . .

'Mother,' she said, 'Brian's packed up and gone.'

It was a child's trick, Naomi was forced to acknowledge, to gain attention. By the look of dismay on Sybil Pemberton's face, it worked.

'Brian's gone?' she echoed. 'Brian——?'

Her mother had been so lost in the desertion of her elder daughter from the responsibilities and joys of motherhood, she appeared even to have forgotten the existence of her grandchild's other parent.

'Brian Westley,' Naomi answered with strained patience. 'You know, Brian—Becky's father.'

'Yes, yes—what about him? You mean he's gone to work?'

Naomi shook her head. 'He's gone, left. There was a note on his pillow.' She searched for and found the note while her mother sat in stunned silence. Sybil read it, then read it again. She turned it over, turned it back.

'No address, nothing about any arrangement to give you money to look after Becky. How could he?'

'He's only doing what Clare did, isn't he?'

Sybil was silent for a few moments, then she brightened just a little. 'You'll have to live on social security, won't you? After all, they'll pay the rent, give you money.'

'Just as if I were a single parent?'

The irony in the situation did not seem to hit home. Sybil nodded eagerly.

'But Mother, I'm not even Becky's mother, just her aunt. I stepped in to help out, not to take over the role of parent. I've got my own life to lead!'

Sybil was silent, staring across the room at her sleeping granddaughter.

'Couldn't you help out, Mum? Couldn't you possibly let me live with you, bring Becky, look after her between us?'

Already her mother was shaking her head.

Naomi put a hand on her mother's lap. 'For Becky's sake? Will you please try asking Dad?'

Sybil sighed. Becky was stirring and making demanding noises as if she were attempting to add her plea to her aunt's. Sybil's attention was caught at once. 'I'll try, Naomi, but I'll have to choose the right moment and the right time. You know how it is with your father. Now, let me hold my little granddaughter and revel in how beautiful she is.'

Later, as it grew dark, Naomi stared out at the back yard of the house. Once, she mused, did children in Victorian dress play in that small area, even getting mud on their clothes? Did their nannies rush to the small boys dusting down their breeches and rub agitatedly at the little girls' short-long skirts?

'Nanny,' she thought, sighing, that's all *I* am really. Worse off even than the young under-privileged women of those days. At least they were paid, despite the fact that it was probably a mere pittance.

When I go into the social security offices to tell them I'm in need of money for myself and the baby I'm caring for, the looks I'll get will tell me what they think of me. Decades may have passed since Victorian times, she reflected, but the social code which dictated that children should have a legal father still persisted beneath the layer of so-called liberality.

Naomi wandered about the room tidying away baby-things. She recalled her mother's overflowing love for her grandchild, then felt a stab of pain at her assumption that her younger daughter, who was blameless in the whole affair, would continue to carry her very young burden, sacrificing her own life and happiness while doing so.

'I'll certainly ask your father, dear, but give me time, won't you?' her mother had pleaded as she had left.

Naomi searched for a name and number in the address book beside the telephone and dialled, waiting for someone to answer. It was a woman's voice.

'Mrs Marlon here,' it said.

'Oh, Mrs Marlon,' even as Naomi spoke she felt her apprehension grow, 'it's about the rental of the flat. I know my friend—Brian—Brian Westley gave notice of ending his tenancy in two weeks' time, but I was wondering if your husband, as landlord, would be willing to renew it in my name.'

There was a heavily-expelled breath in reply.

'You see,' Naomi persisted determinedly, 'I'd have nowhere to go otherwise, and that would be awful because the baby would suffer——'

'Baby? I didn't know Mr Westley had a baby in his flat. Or a woman. Nor did my husband.' Mrs Marlon's self-righteous tone told Naomi how right she had been about her reflection that, basically, public attitudes today had changed little towards unmarried mothers from the dim and not-so-distant past.

'The position is, Mrs Marlon, that I'm just looking after Brian's baby.'

'That's what all the girls who do what you do say. I'm sorry, Miss—er—but I'm sure I speak for my husband when I say "no" to your request. In fact, I should be glad if you'd get out of the place so that it can be cleaned through and offered to someone else.'

'Mrs Marlon,' Naomi persisted, deeply alarmed now, 'I have the means to pay the rent, keep the place neat and clean——'

'That's what they all say. In fact, if you're not out tomorrow—no, we'll make it the day after, to be kind, my husband and his friends will come and put you out.' The receiver clattered in Naomi's ear.

Breathing deeply and compressing her lips, she willed the self-pity away. She'd fight, she would fight them—all of them—until she dropped, which she did, on to the couch. For a moment her head went back, then she reached for the remote control handpiece and found a televised play which she forced her mind to follow, excluding all other thoughts.

After breakfast next morning, she rang Mrs Westley to tell her what had happened.

'Oh, my dear,' Brian's mother exclaimed, 'I'm so sorry about it all. I'd offer you a place here, except—well, you know I'm not fit at the moment and although I love having Becky for a night or two, I just don't think I could manage——'

'Don't worry, Mrs Westley. I'm going to my parents' house. Becky and I can live there until we find a place of our own.'

A few soothing phrases later, Naomi rang off. It took some time to pack all her own belongings and the baby's. When the time came to feed and change Becky, Naomi took the opportunity to relax. In reality, it was only her feet she rested. As Becky grew, so her demands for attention increased.

Having cleaned through the flat, leaving everything where it should be, Naomi took a final look at the place and carried Becky down to Brian's car.

It was well past midday when Naomi drew up outside her parents' house just outside a small East Sussex town. The house was built in the early part of the century but had been well maintained over the years and did not look its age.

Naomi had parked in the drive, hooting twice to let her mother know she was there. It was a signal that had been agreed between them just in case her mother had felt confident enough to allow her to bring Clare's baby into the house for the first time.

Less than a minute later, Sybil Pemberton came hurrying down the steps to the sloping drive. Naomi was puzzled, since she knew her father travelled to London each day from the local railway station.

Sybil was waving her hand, not in welcome but agitatedly. 'He's here, dear,' she said, 'he decided to take the day off to do some digging in the garden.'

'Did you ask him, Mum?'

'I started to, but he told me to stop. He said he wouldn't allow anything of Clare's——'

'Becky's not a *thing*, she's a baby,' Naomi protested heatedly. She opened the car door, winding the window low so to let fresh air into the vehicle. 'Look after her, Mum. I'm going to find my father.'

'For heaven's sake, Naomi,' Sybil called, 'don't quarrel with him about this. He's in the garden . . .' Her daughter was gone.

'Father?' John Pemberton looked round, having plainly recognised his daughter's voice. He straightened, frowning with puzzlement at having been addressed by her so formally.

'I've brought Becky.' Her father opened his mouth to speak, but she went on, 'I want you to let us stay here.'

'Don't you mean live here? Didn't your mother tell you? I said no, and I'm saying no now.'

'Look, Dad,' she watched as he bent to his digging again, 'Brian's gone, vanished into nowhere. I've got no address, no way to contact him.'

John Pemberton threw his fork into the soil. 'That's what I mean by the disgustingly irresponsible ways of the young these days.' He held up his finger. 'And don't you tear me apart with acid comments about ageing parents being out of step with the younger generation. I know all about love, marriage and sex—in that order. I knew about them before you were born!'

Naomi reflected that if the subject matter had not been so serious, she would have laughed at her father's self-evident comment.

Instead, she shook her head. 'And don't you lecture me, either, Dad. Clare's baby isn't mine, but I'm looking after her. Doesn't that show that some of us still have a sense of responsibility?'

Her father looked at her, stretched out his hand and drew her head nearer. Then, in a gesture which was entirely foreign to his undemonstrative nature, he kissed the top of her head.

Naomi smiled up at him, although she knew her father well enough to realise he had not given in yet. 'I'm homeless now, Dad,' she offered winningly. 'Brian's landlord won't let me stay any longer at the flat. Becky's in the car, Dad. She's a beautiful baby. She hasn't got a father or a mother now, so she needs her grandparents' love more than ever.'

He turned on her. 'She's no grandchild of mine. Take her away, take Clare's little b——'

'You mustn't call Becky that,' Naomi exclaimed. 'She's innocent of everything. She was born, because she couldn't help it—could she?—into a hostile world, with hostile people everywhere, a hostile grandfather . . .'

Turning, her voice thick, she ran back along the path, round the house, and slammed into the car, where she found her mother talking to her granddaughter.

'I'll have to find somewhere, even if it's for a couple of nights.'

'He said "no", dear?'

Naomi drew in her lower lip. 'He's the most obstinate, pigheaded man I've ever come across!'

'He feels very strongly about it, Naomi.'

'So do I, Mum, so do I.' She drove off slowly, waving her hand vaguely. 'I'll see you some time. I'll think of something.'

'Let us know your address, dear,' Sybil called after the retreating car. And that, Naomi thought, was the most hurtful comment of all, a kind of verbal washing of hands of the whole matter, disclaiming all responsibility.

For a while, she drove aimlessly along the winding country lanes. They opened out on to a straight length of road with green fields stretching invitingly on each side. Finally she pulled in to a parking bay, lifted Becky out and changed her.

Having fed her and walked around holding her for a while, she returned her to the carrycot. Seated in the driver's seat, Naomi closed her eyes and concentrated on discovering a solution.

Gareth, Gareth, . . . His name came into her head like a whisper on the breeze. Not for a moment had he been absent from her thoughts, not through a single hour of a single day since he had come back into her life. *I'm even willing to marry you,* he had said a few days before. But, her reason whispered, she had thrown his words back in his face.

Starting the engine, she gathered the scattered crumbs of her courage and turned back towards the town in which her parents lived.

This time she drew up at the kerb outside the house she intended to visit, being no more sure of her welcome here than at her parents' house.

It took her a moment to unclench her fingers from the wheel. Applying the handbrake, she made yet another grab at her courage and swung out of the car. This time, she was determined not to leave Becky alone. Lifting her up, she locked the car and made her slow way along the short drive. Having rung the bell, she stood waiting, pressing her cheek against the baby's soft clothing and fighting the shivering which was threatening to take over. For Becky's sake, she told herself, she must remain calm.

The sky had clouded over. Despite the fact that the name of the month indicated that it was summertime, there was a chill wind. Having left her jacket in the car with all her other possessions, she felt in need of warmth.

There was none in the eyes of the man who opened the door. It was not Mr Gill as she had hoped. It was Gareth himself. He was remote and unreachable. He was daunting and handsome and she loved every part of him, but even a single touch from him was barred to her now.

Since he continued to stare at her coldly, she lifted the child she was holding a little higher and asked, 'Please may I come in?'

'I can't think why you should. I told you to get the hell out of my life.'

'There's no one else I can turn to.' She cursed her voice for wavering. He still did not move. 'And—and it's cold out here.' The moment she said the words, the sun broke through and he lifted an unbelieving eyebrow.

'Before I agree, you'll have to think of a better reason than that.'

'You,' she accused, tears springing, 'you're no better

than anyone else! I'd rather sleep out all night in the car than——' She turned to run down the step but his hand on her arm restrained her.

'Come in,' he invited indifferently. 'If you need help, I'll see if I can give it.'

You can give me so much, she thought, you could give me the world, if only . . . Becky made protesting noises, eyeing her host with suspicion. He saw the look and smiled fleetingly and Naomi's heart lurched at the tantalising glimpse of the man she used to know.

'My father's away for a while, staying with a friend on the south coast.'

Naomi nodded, hoping she had managed to hide her disappointment. His father's easy kindliness would have acted as a link between herself and Gareth.

'Sit down, use the couch,' he invited offhandedly. 'There's more room there for you and your child.'

She's not my . . . The words were not spoken. What use would it serve? she thought, sinking into the soft cushions and holding Becky so that she was half-lying on her lap.

Gareth stretched full-length on a low chair, resting his head. His eyes stayed broodingly on her, bringing the colour to her face. It seemed he was prepared to give her no more encouragement.

'Brian's packed up and gone,' she said, lurching straight to the point, too weary to dress up the situation with a careful approach.

'So he's left you?' She did not wince at his bluntness, having expected the comment. 'Not exactly uncommon these days, is it?'

She stormed at him, stung to fury by his shoulder-shrugging manner, 'Need you sit there so smug and self-satisfied? How can you judge me or my actions when your mind is closed, locked and bolted to every explanation I give you of the circumstances?'

He remained as he was, entirely relaxed, legs crossed at the ankles, expressive hands resting on the chair arms. His slacks were creased, his diamond-checked shirt partly unbuttoned, sleeves rolled to elbow height. On his wrist was a stainless steel digital watch, the expanding strap catching down the dark hairs.

The fact that her words had not moved him goaded Naomi still more. 'You wouldn't understand,' she accused, 'the stresses and strains in any relationship between a man and a woman. You wouldn't know about the underlying currents which tug one person one way and the other person another.'

Stopping, dismayed, she thought, What am I saying? I'm implying that there really was, still is, a relationship between Brian and myself. 'I'm—I'm speaking in the abstract,' she added hurriedly, 'objectively, not personally, Brian and I——'

'Are lovers, and parents.' Gareth glanced at the sleeping baby, then straightened in the chair. 'You're talking absolute nonsense, Naomi. Two years ago, I loved you, so much in fact that I wanted to marry you. But I had to make quite sure that you knew what you were doing.'

'So you left me for two years. How you must have loved me!' The bitterness tautened her lips. 'As good as challenged me, in fact, to find someone else.'

For a second, the quick, able fingers tightened on the upholstery. 'And you did, didn't you.' He gestured towards Becky. 'Proof there on your lap.'

He rose and walked about the room. 'No proof, Gareth,' Naomi whispered. 'She's Clare's.'

His jaw hardened, eyes cooled to zero. He walked across to study Becky's features. 'You're lying.' He walked away.

His dismissal of her statement would not go

unchallenged. 'My mother can see Clare in every feature of her face.'

He stood with his back against the door, his hands in his pockets. 'That is a statement you won't allow me to substantiate, will you? You told me it was all a family secret,' he spoke the words with a sneer, 'begged me to keep it to myself. Which I've so far done,' he added carelessly, walking about again.

He paused at last in front of her. 'Anyway, why did you present yourself on this particular doorstep?'

'I told you, there was no one else I could turn to. For—for shelter for myself and the baby.'

He roared to life. 'You think *I* am going to offer shelter to you and your b——' he checked the word with difficulty, 'your *love* child, as they so euphemistically call them these days, when for——' his hand gestured, 'how long, two years? When for nearly two years you've lived with another man, even bearing his child?'

As her agitation at Gareth's accusations increased, so Becky stirred and whimpered. Putting the baby carefully on to the settee, Naomi rose to face Gareth.

Her face was flaming, her heart pounding with anger. 'I've taken more than enough!' she hurled back. 'First, Becky's father walked out, just like that.' She made a slicing action with her hand from one side to the other. 'I've paid the rent, he said, until the end of the month, implying that after that, I could go to hell as far as he was concerned. So I asked his mother for her help. She couldn't do anything because she's not well enough. I'm not blaming her, but that way was barred.'

'Why couldn't you stay on in the flat, taking on the tenancy?'

'Why couldn't I?' she stormed. 'Do you think I didn't try? I'll give you the landlord's phone number and you can speak to his wife, asking why she said her husband wouldn't renew the tenancy in my name. No, don't bother,' came from her sarcastically, 'because the words she used were basically the same as yours.'

She was face to face with him, too close, she thought, because it allowed her to see the way his eyebrows matched the brown of his hair, made her want to press the point of his chin as she had in happier days.

'Now you're going to suggest my parents.' Naomi paused, unnerved momentarily by the way his half-closed eyes were watching her lips move. 'I went there just before I came here. My father turned me—and his grandchild—away. He said exactly the same as you, called her names,' she pointed, 'called that beautiful, innocent baby terrible names! Just like you.' The point of her fingers hit his chest.

Gareth did not move.

Staring at him through rising tears, she accused, 'I'm sick of you, all of you! Call yourselves human beings? You're worse than animals, every single *charitable* one of you!' She moved to the settee, moved back. 'Especially you. You, with your pretence of high principles, your——'

He caught her arms and pulled her close. 'You can stay.'

'Not without the baby.'

'Did I say without the baby?'

Her eyes met his, opening wider, still not quite believing his change of heart. His answering stare told her nothing, but at least the hostility had lessened.

Slowly, she felt the tension leave her, slackening her muscles, weakening her legs. He must have felt the weight of her increase and his arms went round her. They were loose and without tenderness but gave her support when she needed it most.

Involuntarily, her head dropped to rest against his

shoulder. He let it stay as if knowing she needed the feel of a safe harbour to recover from the batterings she had received from the storms in which she had been left to flounder.

Drawing away from him at last, she asked, 'Will your father mind?'

'Not at all. The house is big enough to take the two of you. He'll love having a baby in the house. He's been urging me for a long time now to find myself a wife and produce a grandchild for him.' Gareth removed his arms from her waist. 'Maybe I will one day.' There was no more kindliness in his gaze. 'When I find a woman who can remain faithful to me for more than a few months.'

'Do you take a delight,' she hit out, 'in hitting people where it hurts most? A few minutes ago, I thought I detected a spark of loving kindness in you. Now I know I was mistaken.'

His shoulders lifted and fell. 'Despite your ingratitude, I won't change my mind. You can stay.'

'Who said I was ungrateful?' she cried. 'I appreciate your gesture in offering myself and Becky a roof over our heads. Especially as you dislike me so much.'

'I——' She had stirred his anger again, but he restrained it, hearing the baby's whimpering increasing to a cry.

'Becky darling,' Naomi crouched beside the settee, 'I didn't mean to neglect you.' She lifted the baby, automatically patting her back.

'Is the child hungry?'

She shook her head. 'I fed her in the car.'

'Did you feed yourself?'

'No.' She made as if to go to the door, then hesitated. 'I'm starving hungry.'

For the first time since his return, he laughed, his eyes lighting up. Watching him was like listening to an orchestra rising to a mind-enveloping climax. Her heart sang, her mouth broadening into a delighted smile, matching and surpassing his pleasure.

Their eyes met and Naomi knew that hers, of their own accord, had sent out a message, *please love me again like you did before*. Becky moved in her arms and clung to her jacket. Naomi's eyes, still enmeshed with his, saw his gaze cool to zero. Had he tuned into her mind and read what she was thinking?

'I'm sorry if I'm putting you out—I mean with food and rooms?' she asked without expression.

'If you were I wouldn't have offered you a roof and a bed.' He glanced at an increasingly fretful Becky. 'Where are your things? In your car?'

Naomi nodded, looking around for somewhere to put the baby. Deciding the floor was the safest place, she lowered her to the carpet where the small legs and arms immediately started flailing. Becky opened her mouth wide and yelled. It seemed she had made up her mind to object.

Alarmed, Naomi glanced up at Gareth. As she had expected, he was frowning.

'I'm sorry, but babies do cry sometimes. Would you rather we went away?'

A crack of something approaching fury whipped across his eyes, then it was gone. The sight of it sent Naomi mentally sprawling. Those few shattering seconds told her that no amount of reasoning, nor truth-telling, would ever cancel out her guilt in Gareth's eyes.

'Give me your keys,' was his toneless answer. 'I'll bring in your things.'

'I'll get them myself.' She straightened and took the car keys from her jacket pocket.

He reached out and caught her wrist. Realising his intention, Naomi clutched the keys more tightly, her head lifting, her eyes defying him. Uncaring that he might be hurting her, he forced her fingers open, taking the keys from her.

Doggedly, flexing her sore fingers, Naomi followed him to her car. All the same, she had to stand aside and watch as he opened the boot and extracted two of her three suitcases.

'I'll come back for the rest,' he told her. Naomi nodded, reclaimed the car keys from the boot lock and used them to open the rear door. She lifted out the carrycot, taking it back to the house. On the way, she passed Gareth.

He indicated the carrycot. 'Isn't there a frame for that to stand on?'

'Yes, there is. It's in the boot. Would you mind bringing it?' As they moved on, she called over her shoulder, 'How did you know?'

'My colleagues at the excavation site—some of them had their wives staying with them.' His eyes were like rapier points, thrusting the innuendo home. *You should have been with me, too*, it said.

Naomi put the carrycot on the hall floor, returning to a yelling Becky. Kneeling beside her, Naomi lifted her to rest on her feet. Bare toes curled on the carpet's pile, then uncurled as Naomi allowed the small feet to accept the weight of the rest of Becky's body.

'There's a clever girl,' Naomi encouraged, laughing at Becky's delighted expression.

'Isn't she a bit young for that?' Gareth asked from the door.

'At just over five months? No, as long as I don't keep her in this position for too long. I get advice from the clinic.' Lowering the baby on to her back again, Naomi straightened. 'Is there a clinic near here I can take her to?'

'How the hell do I know?' He lifted himself from the door frame. 'I've never had a baby.'

Naomi greeted his lazy comment with a wide smile.

'Nor a wife to have a child by me.'

It was a statement calculated to remove her smile. It succeeded, and she turned away to hide her despair, straightening Becky's short-sleeved cotton dress. That done, she rose, asking stonily,

'Could you show me the room Becky and I can have?'

Gareth nodded, paused at the door and asked, 'Will she be all right on her own?'

'As long as we aren't too long.'

He nodded again, and Naomi's heart lifted just a little at Gareth's seemingly growing acceptance of Becky's existence and the fact that she had an established gender. He spoke of her as 'she' and 'her' now, instead of just a dismissive 'the child'. Would she, one distant day, find it possible to convince him of her true part in this whole situation?

And if so, would he find it within himself to understand?

It was evening and Naomi looked down at a tired baby. She was, as usual, in the carrycot.

'Haven't you got a proper cot for her?' Gareth had asked as he had shown her a small room next to her own where Becky could sleep.

'Unfortunately, no,' Naomi had told him. 'Brian had been intending to buy one, but he never got round to it. I'll have to use what's left of my savings and buy one secondhand.'

Gareth had made no further comment. He had looked around. 'I hope there's everything here you'll need. Your room is next door. The bed is just covered, so you'll have to make it.'

'I don't mind. It's very kind of you to have us——'

'Cut out the gratitude,' he had sliced across her words, adding sarcastically, 'I accept the situation as inevitable in these enlightened times we live in. Which is why I'm glad I never got myself involved too deeply with a woman.'

As a remark, it was intended to give pain. When she lifted two very brown, very wounded eyes to his, he turned away, going to the door.

'If you want me for anything, or can't find the food and so on, I'll be in my bedroom working. Don't call me for meals—I make my own, or miss out on the eating. It doesn't worry me. If the phone rings, I have an extension in my bedroom.'

She had nodded and he had gone. For the rest of the day there had been no sign of him at all.

By the time she had finished tidying up, the baby was asleep. Closing the door quietly, Naomi returned to her own room with the intention of finding places in which to store her clothes and other belongings. Finding hanging spaces, she put away her coats and dresses, opened another door and discovered a fully-tiled shower room.

It touched her deeply that Gareth should have given her such pleasant living quarters. Losing all desire to carry on with her task, she closed the shower room door and wandered across to the window. Half-sitting on the sill, she stared down into the well-tended garden.

It all came crowding in on her—everything that might have been. If Clare hadn't moved in with Brian, if she hadn't had his baby, if she hadn't run away from them both . . .

There were other and even bigger ifs, she told herself. If she had not taken pity on Brian and especially his baby daughter, if she had not possessed the deep compassion which had led her to take over where Clare had stopped . . .

Moving from the window, she went across to the bed, pushing off her sandals and lying full-length. It was that compassion for which she was now being condemned by the man she loved and respected beyond all others. It was so unfair, she thought, so unfair. Her hands cradled her head on the pillow, the tasteful wallpaper grew blurred.

All those ifs amounted to one thing—without them, she would by now have become Gareth's wife, gone back with him, maybe, to the dig, met the wives and families of the other archaeologists.

And all the time there would have been the security of knowing that she, like the other women, belonged—to a husband who loved her and whose love she returned with equal passion.

There was a tap at the door which opened without her invitation. Naomi lifted herself on to her elbows, startled by Gareth's entry. Her dark brown hair was ruffled, her ribbed sweater twisted from her movements.

He came to stand by the bed. He gazed his fill at the fullness of shape which was emphasised by the summerweight sweater's style, at the curves of waist and thighs to which the folds of her cotton skirt clung.

Finding his scrutiny unnerving, she went to swing her legs to the floor. He bent over her, preventing the movement. With his hands each side of the pillow, she let her head sink back.

'Why did you two-time me, Naomi? All right, so you might have slept with the man for the experience of having fun with another lover. *But did you have to have his baby?*'

His eyes no longer smouldered with a very male desire as they had just now when looking her over. They were flaring and furious, and she could only shake her head in fierce but useless denial.

It was an action which seemed to inflame him even more. His long, strong body joined hers on the bed, pulling her round and into his arms.

'God help me, but I can't resist you. All those

months we spent apart, I thought you were waiting for me to return to you.' In a sharp, infuriated movement he thrust her round on to her back and with his own weight pressed her into the softness of the bedcovers. 'Instead,' he went on, fixing her head still with rigid fingers, 'you got yourself so involved with him you decided to have his child!' He was hurting her jaw, but his hold was such that she was unable to tell him.

His fingers moved, forcing open her teeth so wide and with such strength she could only moan for mercy. He was prepared to give none. His teeth hit hers, his lips closed over her throbbing mouth and her body writhed at his deeply probing exploration.

He was making her swallow the very taste of him as he was drinking from her. Her body was delighting in the feelings he was arousing, and her growing need for him was matched only by his obvious and insistent desire for her.

This was a side of him she had never seen. Always, in the past, he had been tender, especially the night he had brought their love to completion. She was not ready for his unreigned passion and she wanted to tell him so, but he had her mouth in bondage.

His hands were all over her, as ungentle as his mouth. Her stiff fingers clawed at his roughened cheeks and she gathered all her energies to urge him off her. To her immense relief, his apparent wish to punish her seemed slowly to ebb away.

He shifted and lay beside her while she nursed her aching lips.

At last, he said, in a cold, empty voice, 'If I frightened you, I'm sorry. But I'd have expected you by now to have known about every possible aspect of lust.'

'Lust,' he'd called it. But what else did she think he would admit to? That his actions had been motivated by love?

'Gareth?'

After a long time, he answered, 'Yes?'

'If I told you again that Becky isn't my child, would you believe me?'

He lay still for many minutes, so many that Naomi grew cold with tension. An impulse made her seek his hand and rest hers upon it. He gave no indication of objection. Taking courage, she lifted it slowly towards her mouth.

Gareth lay impassively, unresponding. When his fingers—those fingers which had so recently given her such pain—touched her lips, she kissed them, once, twice. Stirring at last, he removed them from her with impatience.

It seemed he no longer wished to lie beside her. He swung from the bed and went across to look out at the darkening garden. She doubted if he really saw a thing.

Lowering her legs to the floor, she pushed her hair back and tugged her ribbed top back into place. Then she watched him, looked with longing at the breadth of his back, the straight strength of his shoulders.

He turned at length and leaned back, casting a shadow across the room. 'Against my better judgment,' he answered her, 'I suppose I could make myself take your word for it.'

Naomi was on her feet and going across to him. Her hands rested on his chest and her hope-illuminated eyes held his. 'You could? I mean, believe what I say about Becky not being mine?'

His hands gripped her rounded cheeks and he studied her smile. 'If you mesmerise me enough with those wide, so bloody innocent-looking brown eyes, I could believe anything you told me—within reason.'

Too overjoyed to notice the added two words, she grasped his shoulders. 'Then, Gareth, do you remember how the other day you offered to marry me?' His expression grew cold, his hands fell to his sides, but she would not allow herself to be discouraged by now. 'Well, I accept, Gareth, with all my heart.'

'And that way, you'd get a father for your baby?'

'You said you believed me—just now, you said you believed me.' There was desperation in her voice. He was slipping out of her grasp. Then she remembered the way he had phrased his capitulation from his position of accuser. *If you mesmerise me enough* . . . More ifs to plague her!

'Ah, but now,' he asserted unpleasantly, 'I've had time to see through the trick it was. Marriage to me would solve your financial problems, give you a roof over your head, offer you security.'

Naomi turned and moved away, sinking on to the bed. 'It's useless, isn't it? I might as well pack our bags, Becky's and mine, and go. I'll find a place somewhere, even if it's only the shed in my father's garden. And if he turns us out from there——'

He strode across the room, catching her arms and lifting her upright to face him. 'I'll marry you. I don't need your verbal blackmail to help me make up my mind. I'll marry you because I can't resist you—I told you that. You, with a face like an angel,' he examined each feature with something near to anger, 'hair like silk,' he traced its outline as it curved around her flushed cheek, 'eyes that don't even flinch when I hurl insults at you!'

His palm ran over her curving shape, lingering on a thrusting breast and coming to rest low down on her hip. Pulling her close, he said roughly, 'Can't you feel my reaction to you? I've only got to look at you to desire you.'

He pushed her from him and regarded her, hands on his hips.

Naomi tugged at the neckline of her ribbed top. 'The baby, Gareth? What about Becky?'

'I'll adopt her, but her own father will have to be traced for his consent.'

'You know what he said before about your adopting her—that he wouldn't allow it.'

'He said that when he was drunk and incapable. Also, he was still living with you.'

'He wasn't——' She stopped herself from adding, 'living with me.'

'Drunk?' Gareth supplied. Accepting the alternative offered, Naomi nodded. 'He was so far gone,' Gareth went on, 'that I'm certain he'd have needed to be put to bed. Am I right?'

Naomi nodded for the second time. She flopped down on to the bed. Gareth was going to marry her! So why was she not rejoicing at the fact? Once again he had been condescending. The other evening her pride had made her reject him. Now her pride had been shattered and ground into dust by the slow, irrevocable disintegration of her life. Most of all, it had been destroyed by the utter contempt in which she was held by the man she loved, and whose wife she would soon become.

CHAPTER FIVE

GARETH opened the bathroom door next morning to be confronted with a dark-haired, dark-eyed fiancée holding a dark-haired, bright-eyed baby.

'Sorry,' said Naomi, starting to turn away. 'We'll wait.'

'I've finished.' Gareth rubbed his cheek to test its smoothness. A small, chubby hand came out to hover vaguely in the direction of where his own fingers had touched.

Naomi laughed, her heart momentarily light. Gareth, who was not unamused himself, commented, 'Good grief, she's got her mother's wicked charm already!'

'Her mother's——?' He means me, of course, she reminded herself dully, he still won't accept that she's Clare's.

He took the hand that was still stretched towards him. Becky made happy noises as the strange man who was not her father looked into her face. Only Naomi could discern the quick frown of pain that snatched away his amusement.

'Make yourself at home,' he remarked casually as he walked away.

His jeans were creased, his shirt flying open with the breeze his own movement created. His hair was still as ruffled as a night's sleep had made it. Yet Naomi was certain she could detect faint pencil-lines of tiredness around his eyes. She longed to be able to stroke them away.

Taking the baby with her, dressed and clean and quiet for a change, Naomi walked along the landing to listen at Gareth's door, trying to hear any sound which would indicate that he was there.

Her ear was straining against the door when it opened and Naomi nearly fell sideways into Gareth's arms. He steadied her, placing one hand behind her back, the other behind the baby's.

'Did you think I had another woman in here with me?' he asked caustically.

Naomi drew away from his touch. 'I thought you might have gone for a jog round the block or something. You might have turned into an exercise fiend in the two years since we parted.'

He smiled unpleasantly. 'I don't know about the "exercise" bit, but I've turned into a fiend.' His insolent sweep of her shape told her more than words.

Trying to ignore the instant response within her to the desire in his look, she went on, 'All I wanted was to ask if I should make your breakfast as well as mine and Becky's. How could I know which room you were in without listening for sounds?'

'You could have knocked or called out,' he commented mildly.

Looking up at him, she could not think of an answer.

'In the old days, you'd have used the full power of your lungs to get me out of a room.'

She shifted the baby, who was growing heavier with each passing month. 'Yelled, you mean? Well,' she frowned, 'there are barriers between us these days, aren't there? Insurmountable ones.' Her free hand found his arm and shook it. 'All in your mind, Gareth, every single one.'

His features had softened, but her words brought the hardness back. 'The evidence is in your arms. She's rather too substantial to have an existence only in my mind.'

Naomi spun round and walked away. 'I'll get my own breakfast,' he called after her.

He discovered her spooning baby cereal into Becky's eager mouth. For a while he watched, appearing amused to find himself the object of the baby's curiosity. At last he moved away, beginning preparations to boil himself an egg.

'By the way,' he informed her, 'I phoned your parents last night and told them you were staying here. Didn't it occur to you that they might be worried?'

'After the way my father turned me away when I asked if Becky and I could stay there, no, it didn't occur to me. Sorry.'

'Your mother was very pleased I let her know. I told her you were too tired to speak to her after the long day you'd had.'

'Thanks for your diplomacy on my behalf. I appreciate it. All the same, it rankles that my mother didn't put up a fight on my behalf, in view of—oh,' she finished, 'it doesn't matter.'

Gareth shrugged, and asked, 'Have you eaten?'

'Not yet.' Naomi was patting Becky's back. 'I'll finish with the baby first.'

'I'm making toast. Like some?'

'Yes, please. That's probably all I'll have.'

'If that's all you eat in the mornings, how do you expect to keep going until the next meal?'

'I manage.'

When he came to take his place at the table, Becky was half-lying, replete, in Naomi's arms.

Gareth started on his egg. 'I still don't understand,' he commented, 'why you didn't breast-feed the child. You used to say that when you had a baby of your own——'

'When I have a child of my own,' she flung at him, 'I'll do just that!' Becky, sensing undercurrents, made crying noises. 'And when I do,' Naomi continued, pacifying her, 'it will be by a man who not only loves me but trusts me!'

Gareth's spoon froze for a second, then he swallowed its contents. Pushing another egg across the table, he advised, 'Have that. It should help to ease your hunger and your temper.'

For a moment Naomi ignored him, then her eyes slid round to look at his offering. It was covered with an egg-cosy and she was tempted. 'It's yours. No, thanks.'

'I cooked it for you, along with some toast.' He shifted the toast-rack to her side.

Her eyes met his, hers unsure and suspicious of his motives, his daring her to refuse.

The aroma of the toast had titillated her taste buds. There was no doubting that she was hungry. 'That was kind of you,' she gave in stiffly.

'Anything to keep my fiancée's tongue sweet,' he commented, his eyes lazy, 'and her figure in trim. She has a lot to offer. I'd hate it to have diminished by the time we marry.'

Her lips compressed, tight-reining her anger. It was all she could do with a now-restless baby in her arms. Propping up her back with a low pillow, she lifted the carrycot from the floor and on to its frame.

Gareth watched, saying, 'If you'd told me, I'd have done that for you.'

'Thanks, but I've done it so many times and for so long, I'm used to it.'

Returning to the table, she took some toast before tackling the egg.

'How long, Naomi?' he asked softly.

Swiftly she looked up. Was there a question in his mind at last? Since it was impossible to read his expression, she shrugged. 'Long enough.'

He finished his coffee and rose from the table. 'You'll need a high chair for the baby, won't you?'

'In a couple of months, probably. Why?'

'Tell me and I'll buy one.'

'Thanks, but I think that will be my responsibility, don't you?'

His chair grazed back on the floor covering. His voice matched the sound. 'Since you're going to become my wife, no, I don't.'

He was at the door. Naomi turned. 'If I need you, Gareth——'

'By heaven,' he rasped, 'I'm going to make you *need* me before many days have passed!'

Refusing to let her pain register on her face, she continued as if he had not spoken, 'If there's anything I can't find, for instance, where will you be?'

'In my room, as usual. Or the one next to it. I keep my collection in there.'

'Your bits and pieces, artefacts from the dig, all neatly labelled, of course?'

'Of course,' he answered, throwing back her sarcasm, 'despite the fact that I've had to manage without the help of my irreplaceable assistant, Pam Hatton.'

Naomi quelled the thrust of jealousy that hit her at his softened tone of voice as he spoke the name and asked, 'Is she the person who answered the phone that day I rang you back at the excavation site and you refused to speak to me?'

'She is.'

'I suppose she's your girl-friend?' The question was blunt, but Naomi was in no frame of mind to soften it.

'Carry on supposing. Do you think I'd tell you?'

Swinging round to face him, she declared. 'Yes, I do, since we're going to be married.'

'You keep your secrets, so I shall keep mine. Right?'

She nearly ran after him and battered his back until he told her. Becky made a noise of protest at the raised voices and Naomi went across to her, distracting her by pushing along the large beads which were stretched across the carrycot.

It was while Becky was having her afternoon sleep that Naomi decided to storm Gareth's stronghold and ask him to clarify his plans for their future. In the hours that had passed since breakfast, she had seen no sign of him.

Having knocked on his bedroom door, she prepared herself for a long wait, only to be told to stop playing the self-effacing servant and come straight in.

Even his back as he sat writing revealed how short-tempered he was. He did not turn from his work, continuing to write.

'Longhand?' she asked, watching over his shoulder.

He threw down his pen. 'You know damned well I can't type.'

'Which the irreplaceable Miss Pam Hatton can, of course?'

'Of course.'

'Which I can do, also. You know that from when I used to work in your department at the university.'

'Which also is how I came to know the beautiful Miss Naomi Pemberton. And, like a fool,' he caught her wrist and swung her round and on to his lap, 'fell headlong in love with her.'

Naomi struggled to sit upright and remove herself even as he eased her relentlessly backwards across his thighs. He blocked easily her every attempt to escape. His hand supported her head which was hanging back, but it was not an action taken to ease the strain on her neck muscles.

His jaw was hard, pulling at his half-smiling lips. 'I could do what I liked with you, couldn't I?' His other hand stroked her thighs, moving upwards to rest on her stomach. 'To me this is familiar ground. I've been over it all before. Two years ago when we were in love, since then in all the dreams I had about you.'

He smiled as she gasped at the audacity of his invading hand, and let her head fall. She tried in vain to lift herself, unable to stand the throbbing arousal his hand was causing inside her.

'Please, please, Gareth,' she moaned, 'stop touching me!'

Unceremoniously she was pulled upright, but her longing to be loved by him would not let her make another bid for freedom. Her head lolled to his shoulder, then slid lower until her cheek rested against the unbuttoned opening of his shirt. Her fingers bunched the fabric, giving her a hold to steady her.

'I could take you now, couldn't I, my beautiful cheat?' he taunted.

Naomi stiffened, pulled upright and said, aghast, 'You call me that when before long you'll be my husband?' This time she slipped easily from his hold. With moist palms, she brushed back her hair and wished she could with the same ease brush away the ache of desire he had awoken.

'I came to see you to talk about our—our future together. But you can forget it, forget you ever said you'd marry me. You can even forget my existence.'

By now she was at the door, but in a few strides he was swinging her from it and barring her way. 'Okay, I'll stop work and we'll talk.'

Sinking on to a low chair, she sat forward, elbow on knee, hand to her cheek. Despondently, she stared at nothing, looking inward. I'm caught in a trap, she thought, everything's closed in on me without my even noticing. I was so busy looking after Becky . . .

'If there were any possible alternative,' she declared, 'I would take it rather than marry a man who looks on me with the contempt that you do!'

Gareth sat at his desk, swinging his chair so that he faced her, but it seemed he had nothing to say in answer to her statement. Clasping his hands behind his head, he swivelled gently from side to side. He too was staring at nothing in particular. All the activity appeared to be taking place inside his head.

After a while he remarked, still without focusing on her, 'You came to talk to me. What about?'

Her shoulders lifted and fell. 'About the date of the wedding, about your suggestion of adopting Becky.'

'When all obstacles are removed, I'll keep my promise and adopt her.'

'Which means I'll have to try and discover Brian's whereabouts.'

'I could put an agency on to that, if you wish.' He was looking at her now.

'I'd rather not, unless it's really necessary. I'll——' She glanced up at him, seeing with a shock that he was watching her. It was impossible to fathom the strange look in his eyes, but it made her shiver as if, under the power of his thought, she had turned into a ghost.

She guessed that he had allowed his imagination to transport him back to the days when they had been in love, to the time he had taken her and made her his.

Dragging her own thoughts back to the present, she went on, 'I'll have a talk with my mother.' She stopped abruptly, hoping he would not ask what her mother could do to help that he couldn't. Although the question did not come, she explained with a too-quick smile, 'A girl likes to discuss her problems with her mother.'

'As Becky will one day with you?'

'Well, I hope——' He had caught her out. How could she tell him that she was so fond of her niece, having looked after her for so long, that she almost did regard her as her own daughter? Having no other explanation to make about her response, she was silent.

'It's a good thing, isn't it,' he commented, lowering his hands and folding them across his chest, 'that I never had a sister. She would have had no mother to talk to, since my mother left my father while I was quite young.'

'I remember you told me your parents were divorced.'

'So you do remember? My father has only recently begun to get over it, although it happened years ago.'

'But you've never got over it.' Again, she looked up at him, finding his hard, handsome face regarding her. 'Which is why you hate me so much for what you imagine I've done.'

'Imagine?' He got up and walked about, hands in pockets. 'Isn't Becky sufficient evidence?'

'You've said that before.' Her voice had risen. 'Becky's Clare's,' she cried, hammering the chair arm with her fist. 'Why won't you believe me? Do you think I'd marry a man, especially you, because I need a roof for myself and the baby, because I've got no other way of ensuring we get the secure future we need so much?'

'After the way my mother treated my father, I'd believe anything of any woman.'

Her eyes strained upward to meet his. 'Your mind's so warped on the subject of women, it's beyond saving! All right, I'll say whatever you want me to say. Becky's mine, Brian Westley's the father.' She stood confronting him, white-faced, defiant. 'Now what are you going to do? Turn us both out of your house? Put us on the streets?'

Gareth moved round the table on which he had been writing, going to a clothes chest and opening a drawer. When he turned, Naomi saw that he held a small box. Flipping open the velvet-covered top, he returned to stand near her.

'Give me your left hand.'

She kept it tightly clenched.

He lifted it, prised open her fist and slipped the ring on to her engagement finger. Naomi gazed at the pure beauty of the diamond and wanted to put it to her lips.

'You needn't have bothered,' she asserted. 'Our marriage will be meaningless. You won't want to make love to me. In your eyes, I deserted you just like your mother did your father.'

He snapped the box shut and slipped it into his pocket.

Naomi stared at the ring. 'Feeling as you do about the unfaithfulness of women, I can't think why you gave me two years to make up my mind. You said I might find someone else——'

'Which you did,' he broke in, 'and felt so deeply for him you had his baby.'

'Go on. And now he's left me, which is no more than I deserve, behaving as irresponsibly as I did. Why don't you say it?'

He shrugged. 'It's all been said.'

'Couldn't I, on those grounds alone,' she persisted, 'say now how much I hate men and that I'll never trust them again?'

'You could. If so, we shall go well together, each expecting nothing of the other. If either of us is unfaithful we'll both understand.'

'How could you be so cynical?' she whispered. 'If I marry you, I'll never leave you.'

'Of course you won't. Materialistically speaking, you'd have too much to lose, wouldn't you?'

Her large accusing eyes found his. 'At this moment, I dislike you intensely, and in the course of our marriage, I have no reason to expect my opinion of you to change.' She saw his anger ignite, but she didn't care. 'Don't expect me ever to sleep with you, will you?'

Gareth gripped her arms. 'You'll sleep with me, have no doubts about that. Once, I could have taught you the ways of love. Soon I'll teach you the ways of a man who lusts after a woman.' His voice lowered on a note of threat, 'With no love at all mixed in.'

Naomi fought free, rubbing her arms, raising pain-filled eyes to his.

It was Saturday morning and Naomi had taken a chance on her father being out. At weekends, she knew from experience, he often called on his friends.

Lifting a wakeful Becky out of the carrycot, she locked Brian's car and walked up the drive, aiming for the back door. It stood open as her mother worked in the kitchen.

It was Becky who drew Sybil Pemberton's attention to them. At the sound of a throaty baby noise, Sybil turned and put a hand to her chest.

'You gave me such a start,' she remarked, drying her hands and hurrying across to take her granddaughter's waving, outstretched arm. 'You little darling,' she commented, and placed a resounding kiss against the round, full cheek. 'Can I take her?' Naomi gave Becky to her grandmother and smiled at her mother's radiant face.

'I can see you in her, Mum,' Naomi commented encouragingly.

'Maybe,' Sybil conceded, 'but she's nearly all Clare. Naomi,' she was frowning now, 'how could Clare walk off and leave this beautiful baby of hers?'

Naomi shook her head, having no answer. She went to the door. 'I wanted to make sure that Father was out.' Sybil nodded. 'So could you hold her a few minutes while I get the carrycot frame in from the car?'

Naomi was back quickly, opening out the folded frame. 'I need it in case Father comes back,' she stated with a smile, 'to make a quick getaway.'

Sybil's smile turned quickly into a frown. 'If only he'd take a peep at his little granddaughter,' she sighed, handing Becky over and watching while Naomi settled her down for her morning sleep.

'Dare I put her in the garden? Dad wouldn't creep in, would he? I mean, he usually makes enough noise to waken a herd of elephants. That would give me sufficient warning to push her down the sideway while he comes in the front door.'

Sybil agreed and watched again as her younger daughter eased the carrycot, now on wheels, down the steps. When Naomi returned, her mother commented, 'You're doing wonders with her, darling. One day Clare will thank you.'

'Will she?' Naomi's question was spoken indifferently. 'Mum, I really came because—well, there are some important things I'd like to discuss with you.'

'Yes, dear, of course.' Sybil removed her apron, curiosity hurrying her movements. 'Would you like coffee? No? Let's come into the other room, then, shall we?'

Naomi settled into the armchair she had come, over the years, to regard as her own. Now she had been virtually banned from the house by her unrelenting father, not through her own, but her sister's callousness, the feel of its hard-wearing fabric under her fingers held nostalgia.

In that chair, she had curled up and read books and dreamed—of the man she would one day marry, how she would meet him since he must have been, even then, somewhere in the world. She had been a schoolgirl, just into her teens. Four years would have to pass before Gareth Gill and his father moved into the district.

'Well, dear,' her mother's voice jogged her to awareness, 'what is it you want to talk to——' She gasped, pointing. 'That ring—whose is it?'

Naomi twisted it. 'Mine.' She held it out for her mother's inspection.

'It's really beautiful, darling, but who—why . . .?'

'Gareth, Mother. We're going to be married, but don't tell Father, will you?'

Sybil nodded, asking, 'Naomi, how did he know you'd accept? I mean—well, the ring, it fits so beautifully.'

'Yes,' she frowned down at it, 'I don't know how he guessed my size so well.'

'You were friendly with him, weren't you, before he went off to live and work in York.'

Friendly. Naomi thought. If only my mother knew how 'friendly' we were!

'Is that why you went to him, dear, knowing that he loved you and wouldn't turn you away?'

'It's a bit more complicated than that, Mother.'

'Complicated? I don't see why.' Sybil's eyes opened with alarm. 'What about Becky? Who's going to look after her when you're married?'

'Do you think I ought to refuse Gareth's offer for Becky's sake?'

Mrs Pemberton appeared to miss the sarcastic twist to her daughter's question. 'No, no, of course not, but—Naomi, I can't be expected at my age . . . nor your father.'

Naomi closed her eyes, hoping she would manage to hold on to her temper. What about at my age, she thought, with all my life in front of me?

Opening her eyes, she looked hard at her mother. 'Gareth still thinks Becky is mine.'

Sybil seemed totally confused. Her hand went shakily to her hair, then descended to her lap. 'That's a good thing, then, isn't it?'

Naomi felt she could take no more. 'Good thing, Mother? Do you know what you're saying?' She was sitting upright, grasping the chair arms.

'Not really, dear, I . . .' Sybil smiled, as if she had found a solution. 'I give you permission to tell Gareth the truth. If your father's angry, I'll tell him it's all right, because Gareth will soon be one of the family.' She seemed to realise the perils implicit in spreading the truth. 'As long as he doesn't tell his father.'

Naomi had been shaking her head while her mother had been speaking. 'It's no good, Mum. I've already told Gareth. Sorry I did it without your permission, but it made no difference. Gareth didn't believe me. He said I was only using Clare to clear myself of blame. He thinks I was living with Brian, too—in the real sense, if you know what I mean.'

Instead of finding horror on her mother's face, she saw relief.

Sybil sighed. 'That's all right, then. It clears Clare, doesn't it? She's a struggling young actress. However could she make it to the top with the label "unmarried mother" hanging round her neck?'

'They call it "single-parent family" these days, Mum,' Naomi informed her dryly.

'It makes no difference, does it? If she were an established actress, it wouldn't matter so much. They can do outrageous things and their fans don't mind, so the papers say. But Clare's got quite a way to go yet.'

'At least Brian loves his baby daughter.'

'You surprise me, dear. He walked out on her, didn't he?'

'He could hardly have taken her with him, could he?' Naomi could not stop herself from smiling at her mother's strangely mixed-up arguments. 'How could he earn money if he had to stay at home all day with a young baby?'

'Which is just what I mean about Clare, dear.'

To which, Naomi felt despondently, there was nothing to add.

'Gareth is willing to adopt Becky, Mother.'

'Why, that's wonderful! It solves all the problems, doesn't it?'

'From Clare's point of view, maybe. Look, Mum,' Naomi rallied, 'even if things happen as planned and Gareth goes ahead with the adoption, there are important steps to be taken—like getting Brian's consent.'

'I don't think that's really necessary, dear, but Clare should be asked. She gave me her address in confidence.' Sybil smiled. 'I know her answer already. It will be "yes".'

'You don't sound very put out at the idea of your daughter giving away her baby, Mum, yet you're the baby's grandmother!'

'Oh, but it wouldn't really be giving her away, would it? I mean, it would all be in the family. And I know how much you love her.'

Naomi tried not to let her exasperation show. 'All the same, Gareth insists that Brian gives his consent. Don't forget he thinks Becky's parents are Brian and myself.'

Sybil looked less sure of herself. 'I suppose I'll have to contact Clare and hope she knows where Brian's gone. Otherwise, I suppose the marriage—your marriage—won't take place?'

Naomi considered her ring. 'I don't know, I just don't know.'

There was the sound of footsteps crossing the driveway. Sybil shot to her feet. 'It's your father, dear.'

Hurriedly, Naomi collected her belongings and ran outside, her mother following. 'I'll contact Clare,' she whispered. 'Her address is still the same. She said she'd write to me if it changed. Now, do hurry, dear!'

Naomi planted a quick kiss on her mother's cheek, grasped the handle of the carrycot and hurried round the side of the house. To her alarm, she saw that her father had decided to use the kitchen door rather than the front entrance.

He stood stock still in her path. Anger had turned his face scarlet, but she pushed the carrycot until it almost touched his legs. He shouted, 'I thought I told you——'

A yell from Becky stopped him immediately. Slowly his feet took him round to the side of the carrycot. He stared down unbelievingly at the face so like his elder daughter's. Two small arms were waving about, two perfectly-shaped lips were open to let out a second shriek.

It was so piercing, Naomi covered her ears.

'By heaven,' Becky's grandfather exclaimed, 'I wouldn't have believed it possible! She's got her mother's temper and her mother's powerful lungs!'

'Excuse me, Dad.' Naomi pushed on. 'Her mother's sister is in a tearing hurry. 'Bye for now.'

Leaving her father staring after her, she made for the car.

Naomi lifted the baby into her arms, leaving the carrycot in the hall. There were voices coming from the kitchen, both male.

While Naomi hesitated, Becky made their presence known. Opening the kitchen door, she found Gareth and his father seated at the table, drinking coffee from mugs. One pair of grey eyes looked astonished, the other annoyed.

The father stood up, staring at the baby. The baby stared uninhibitedly back. Gareth asked irritably, 'Where have you been?'

'To see my mother. I would have told you, but you disappeared up to your room. I assumed it was to work, so I didn't disturb you. I was just longer than I thought I'd be, that's all. Hallo, Mr Gill. Nice to see you back.'

'You, too, Naomi. What's this little mite doing

here?' Half amused, he turned to his son. 'Know anything about this, Gareth?'

'Oh, no, Father, you don't lay that little lot on my doorstep!'

His frown deepening, Eddie Gill asked, 'Yours, Naomi?'

Naomi shook her head. 'Mine to look after, Mr Gill, but——'

'I'm adopting her,' Gareth interrupted expressionlessly. 'Did I forget to tell you? Naomi and I are going to be married.'

His father looked delighted, his careworn face creasing into a smile. 'So you're going to give me a daughter-in-law at last! That's grand. Two years ago, I had hopes. I don't know what happened between you and I don't suppose you're going to tell me.' He reached out and kissed Naomi's cheek.

The baby made a 'me-too' noise and Mr Gill laughed, placing a light kiss on the second cheek, chubbier than the first. 'I don't know whose she really is, but she's all female, isn't she, asking for a kiss!' Chuckling, he sat down.

'She's not mine, Mr Gill.' He looked at her, bewildered. 'She's Clare's baby, but Gareth won't believe me.' Naomi approached Gareth's father. 'Do you believe me, Mr Gill? Do you really think she looks like me?'

Eddie Gill stood up again, taking the baby's hand and searching her features. 'She's the image of you, dear. That's all I can say about it.' He subsided on to his chair. 'Don't draw me into your argument, quarrel or whatever it is.'

'Everyone sees who they want to see in Becky's face,' Naomi returned, her voice rising.

Eddie Gill was shaking his head. 'I was impartial, dear. It's just that, to me, the resemblance hits you.'

Gareth tipped back his head to drink from his mug,

his eyes narrowed on Naomi. She threw him back a staring challenge. *Prove it*, was her silent message. No, that's your prerogative, was his equally silent answer.

They were seated, that evening, in the living-room. Father and son had been talking as Naomi entered. Tired after cooking the meal and clearing away, even with help from the men, she looked around for a place to sit.

Gareth was on the couch. Mr Gill watched Naomi with a smile, waiting for her to take the empty space beside his son. Gareth watched, too, but his smile held no pleased expectancy. In itself, it was a kind of come-if-you-dare look, giving her no alternative but to do just that.

His father leaned forward. 'Show me the ring, dear.' He examined it closely. 'I've seen it before, haven't I?'

'I bought it two years ago.' Gareth's face was like a blank page as he turned it to the girl beside him.

'So that's why it fits me so well!' Naomi exclaimed.

'Why didn't you give it to her then, son? All this would have been avoided if you had.' He indicated the upper floor where Becky slept.

'I had to be sure,' Gareth answered shortly.

'Maybe you did, maybe you didn't. What happened between your mother and me—well, the faults weren't all on her side, but we won't go into that.' Eddie Gill scratched his head. 'Look what did happen when you two were apart, yet you're still marrying her.'

The unreadable face turned to Naomi again. 'She knows why.'

His father shrugged. 'Well, perhaps she knows her own mind now.' Naomi fidgeted at the way they were discussing her. Gareth's father pressed, 'Where's the bloke who—you know what I mean.'

'Fathered it,' Gareth filled in coldly. 'He's left her.'

'Packed up and went, just like that?' Naomi nodded. 'I know how it feels, dear.' There was a long pause.

'What would you say, Mr Gill,' Naomi broke the silence, 'if I told you I'm truly not Becky's mother?'

Eddie Gill looked at his son uncomfortably. 'I really think you'd better leave me out of it, dear. You're marrying Gareth. He'll take care of you both.'

Naomi let her head rest back on a cushion, closing her eyes. She was in a trap, a locked room with a lost key. She felt a hand take hers. At once, her head came up and she tugged to free herself.

If her fiancé's father had not been present, she would have accused him of being two-faced in pretending to care about what happened to her, or to Becky.

'You can live here when you're married,' Eddie informed them, but it was Naomi to whom he addressed the words. His son seemed to know. 'I'm packing my things and leaving.'

Naomi felt deeply concerned. 'But Mr Gill, you can stay. It's your home. And anyway, my marriage to Gareth won't be a—well, a proper one. He's only taking Becky and me on out of pity.'

'Is that what you think?' Gareth responded softly, his hand stroking the length of her bare arm. His touch was so light and so potent, Naomi's skin grew cold, yet at the same time it burned.

'No need for me to stay, dear,' Mr Gill was saying. 'I've just been telling Gareth I'm getting married again. He knew it was on the cards.'

Eddie Gill was only in his mid-fifties, as Naomi knew. All the same, the news came as something of a shock. She managed a smile while trying to sort out the consequences of Mr Gill's removal from the house. Would he want to sell, which would mean Gareth would perhaps look for a flat somewhere? Would he still continue with plans for their own marriage? Caring as little as he did about her, she would not blame him, in the changed circumstances, if he abandoned her.

Naomi remembered to say how pleased she was to hear the news. It was true, she thought. Gareth's father had spent so many unhappy years mourning his dead marriage, he deserved now to find happiness.

Gareth spoke, breaking into her wandering thoughts. 'My father is handing over the house to me. I'll be responsible for the money side, plus everything else, but it will still remain my father's property.'

'I thought it best,' Mr Gill put in. 'One day, you and Gareth might want to buy something better for yourselves, especially when you start adding to your family. The lady I'm marrying has a little place on the south coast. It's quite big enough for the two of us.'

Naomi nodded understandingly.

'I want you to come with me this evening to your parents' place,' Gareth informed her. As her head swung round, he added, 'It's all right, my father's agreed to babysit.'

Naomi sent a brief and smiling 'Thanks' in Mr Gill's direction, then asked Gareth, frowning, 'Why do you want to see my parents?' The reason came to her and she exclaimed, 'You're going to ask my father's permission?'

'That was my intention. Do you think he'd like it if I didn't?'

Naomi smiled fleetingly. Gareth made an abrupt movement and she felt his thigh brush against hers. 'He certainly would mind, being a traditionalist to the core. Don't worry, he'll be only too pleased to get me off his hands.' Eddie moved in his seat. Gareth's legs seemed to withdraw from all contact with her.

Again, his action held an unmistakable meaning and she realised just what conclusions the two men would come to at her spontaneous and unguarded statement. She went cold inside, and this time it was she who separated herself from the man beside her. He looked pointedly at the empty space between them and shrugged.

'Does that baby of y——, that Becky-imp upstairs take kindly to babysitters?' Eddie asked.

'She'll give you no trouble, Mr Gill,' Naomi answered, pretending she had not noticed his hasty re-phrasing of the question. 'If she wakes, it won't be until the early hours. Anyway, we'll be back long before then.'

'I shall be taking you somewhere for a drink,' Gareth remarked. 'It's the least we can do as a celebration—toasting our coming marriage.'

'You could have taken her for a meal. Why not make use of Becky's grandparent-to-be while I'm here?'

It was a loaded question, but Eddie was completely unaware of the fact. Naomi and Gareth exchanged glances. His was cool-to-freezing, hers held denial and a bitter defiance.

'Thanks, Mr Gill,' she said, dragging her gaze from that of her fiancé, 'but I'm too full from the evening meal we had to eat any more.' She turned back to Gareth. 'Nor do I want to drink to our engagement. Thanks for the thought,' she added carelessly.

Rising, she pulled down her summerweight top, her glance drawn back unwillingly to meet Gareth's uninhibitedly interested eyes. Going to the door, she announced, with her back to Gareth to hide the colour his scrutiny aroused, 'I'll do my face and hair. I won't bother to change out of my jeans since we're only going to my parents.'

Clicking the door into place, she crossed to the stairs. The sitting-room door had opened and closed and she glanced down with a ready smile, having assumed it was Mr Gill come to ask her about Becky's needs. Instead, it was Gareth, his mood dark, sending her smile flying and Naomi racing to the top of the stairs.

He caught her there and swung her round, holding her arms. 'I'm taking you for a drink, not just to your parents'. So you can "bother" to change these things,' he reached down and grasped a handful of fabric which clung to her thigh, 'and put on a skirt so that I can see your legs. As an engaged man I have rights, as your one-time lover I have even more rights.'

His eyes dropped to look at her swelling fullness. They held a male desire, not love, hurting her sensibility, while the intimate hold of his grip on her thigh lit the fuse of her indignation. At the same time it excited and she wanted to cling instead of twist away, but separate herself she did, with no little pain to her body and her feelings.

Bending to rub the inner flesh of her leg where his fingers had held the fabric so tightly, she flashed up at him, 'I'll do as you say. I'll wear a skirt,' she was almost in her room, 'a long one so you won't even be able to see my ankles!'

His foot was in the door. 'Do that if you like, but don't blame me if you feel out of place among all the other women.' He closed the door before her thrusting hand could reach it.

When she re-entered the sitting-room nearly thirty minutes later, Naomi shot a look at Gareth which said, 'criticise me now'. He had been talking to his father and stopped in mid-sentence. The father's eyes followed the son's.

The dress Naomi had chosen to wear was a vivid pink in colour. It hugged her throat with a stand-up, pleated frill and was secured below it by a bow. A deep vee-shaped frill met at the buttoned front, while the short sleeves were as simply styled as the roll-pleated skirt falling from a neat waistline. The entire dress was semi-transparent and followed faithfully the line of her figure.

Gareth stood up, and his father began to follow, but

only made it halfway. Naomi smiled and shook her head, indicating that there was no need. Then, with a lift of her chin, she challenged her fiancé,

'Do I pass the censor, or would you be ashamed to introduce me to the wives of your academic colleagues?'

He went over to her, catching her shoulder roughly. 'You know damned well how attractive you are. As for my colleagues' wives, you'd beat the lot in looks.'

'But their morals are so much better than mine, aren't they? They don't have babies born out of wedlock hanging round their necks? Their husbands' morals are impeccable, too.' She gave him a sideways glance, her finely-pencilled eyebrows raised. 'Better than yours, even?'

He jerked her chin round. 'If my father weren't here——'

'Forget about me, lad. Put her across your knee if that's how you feel.' Eddie chuckled. 'She's a cheeky minx, that girl you've chosen. I always did think you were a fool to let her slip out of your hands a couple of years ago.'

'Slip out of his hands, Mr Gill?' Naomi retorted. 'He *pushed* me away! He'll tell you otherwise, but I think it was really to leave the field clear for his own activities with the opposite sex.'

Eddie's chuckle turned into laughter. 'She's being really saucy now, son! I should take her round to her parents at the double, if I were you. She might behave better there!'

'Come on.' Gareth caught her arm again. He lifted his hand to his father and pulled Naomi behind him, waiting impatiently while she grabbed a coat from the hall cupboard.

Pulling on the coat, she followed him to his car. It was large, silver-grey and sleek. Pausing while he opened the door for her, she gave him a wide, infectious smile. He did not smile back, but in his eyes she swore she caught a flicker of indulgence.

As he settled into the driving seat, he commented to the darkening view through the windscreen, 'Living a little has put a bite in your tongue.'

Her anger shot into play like the blade of a pen-knife attached by a spring. '*Lived* a little? I haven't lived in the past few months, I've just existed. Looking after a growing baby, a flat, and someone else's boy-friend couldn't by any stretch of the imagination be called living!'

Gareth fired the engine and drove slowly out of the driveway. 'Hardly someone else's boy-friend when he fathered your child. He may be now, of course, having left you.' He left the question in the air. Naomi let it hang. There was no way of dealing with it satisfactorily.

After a while, she remarked, 'I hope my parents are in. They have so many friends, they could be out socialising.'

'They'll be in. I rang your mother earlier today.'

'Thanks for telling me,' she retorted. 'Did you inform her of the reason for our visit?'

'She didn't ask and I didn't enlighten her.'

'I told her this morning you were going to marry me. She was delighted.'

'Like mother, like daughter,' he commented laconically.

Her head shot round. 'I was not delighted.'

He mimicked her, 'I accept your offer, Gareth, with all my heart.' Viciously he braked, having almost driven past her parents' turning.

'That was because——' It was useless finishing the sentence. He wouldn't believe her if she told him that it was because she loved him.

Sybil opened the door wide, hugging Naomi and kissing Gareth's cheek. 'You're no stranger,' she told him, her bright face creasing in a smile. 'But it's so nice to see you again.'

John Pemberton was at the living-room door, his hand outstretched to the tall, brown-haired young man who towered above him. Naomi removed her coat and hung back in the hall, detaining her mother.

'You will tell Gareth the truth, Mum—please? It isn't a secret any more. I told you I told him the real situation, but he didn't believe me. Will you and Dad convince him? He'll accept it from you.'

'How pretty you look, dear. Is that a new dress? I haven't seen it before.'

'Mother, please . . .'

John Pemberton called from the living-room. 'Be sociable and join us, you two ladies. This isn't the right time for woman-talk!'

Sybil guided her reluctant daughter to join the men. 'Gareth, I've seen the ring. Naomi told me.'

'Told you what?' John Pemberton was frowning, brushing his already neatly-combed hair from his forehead.

Naomi thought with a touch of acid, So Mother's actually managed to keep something to herself. It must have been an effort since she usually blurts out everything to Dad.

'I thought this was just a friendly visit,' John commented, sinking back into his favourite chair and indicating that Gareth should use the settee.

Swiftly, Naomi occupied her mother's chair, waiting for her to sit next to Gareth. Sybil hesitated, looking from one to the other. Gareth summed up the situation at a glance, gave Naomi a mock-menacing look and clicked his fingers at her. Then he pointed, stabbing the air over the seat beside him.

Holding back stiffly for a few seconds to signify her freedom of choice, she obeyed, partly to give her mother her own chair, but mainly because every particle of her body was straining to sit beside him. Lifting and turning her head sharply at his mocking smile, she clasped her hands in her lap, only to find his hand reaching out and taking firm possession of one of them.

All the time, John Pemberton looked on with amusement and also a large degree of admiration for the brown-haired, cleft-chinned and plainly strong-minded man who had two years ago been accepted as almost a member of the family. 'Almost' was the important word, since the young man had disappeared into limbo, taking himself off to England's north country. Then had come that business with Clare . . .

'Mr Pemberton,' John snapped out of his deep contemplation, turning to the subject of them, 'your daughter and I are going to be married. I hope you have no objection?'

John showed himself to be a little taken aback by the abrupt statement, having expected at least a request for permission. So many traditions had been trodden down, he seemed to be reflecting—Naomi was reading with complete accuracy her father's every expression—it was a pity that even the courtesy of speaking initially to the girl's father had been abandoned. But at least, on this occasion, his future son-in-law had spoken to him without first producing the next generation. Not like Clare's unfortunate little indiscretion.

Clare? Gareth surely didn't know about Clare? Had Naomi told him?

Naomi smiled without amusement as she detected her father's panic, saw his darting glance. 'Yes, Father,' she offered. 'Gareth knows about Clare. You see, I told him.'

She almost felt her mother start up from her seat with alarm, while her father actually left his. 'What about Clare?' he bluffed, red in the face. 'She's doing well in Manchester—got the star part in the latest offering by the repertory company she joined.'

Naomi looked at her mother, whose guilt sat on her features like a naughty child who had been caught sampling party cakes in advance. Pleasure was there, too, pride in her elder offspring's achievements sitting side by side with a bad twinge of conscience.

Gareth glanced at the girl beside him. Her hand had grown limp in his, her head drooping as she strove to hide her desolate, let-down feeling.

'You have no objection, then, Mr Pemberton,' Gareth reminded Naomi's father gently, 'to my making Naomi my wife?'

'Your wife?' John Pemberton hurriedly collected his straying wits. 'None at all, Gareth, absolutely none. The baby,' he recalled Becky's existence with apparent shock, 'what will you do with her? I mean, Naomi wouldn't like to lose her. She's so fond of the child, I'm sure she wouldn't want to let her go.'

'Go where, Mr Pemberton? I intend adopting Becky, then she will belong to both of us.'

John's eyes sought those of his wife. 'Adopt? You adopt her? Sybil, what do you say? Would it be the best solution?'

Sybil glanced at her daughter, whose hand was back clasping the other, whose head was resting against the couch.

'Solution?' Sybil Pemberton queried. 'Yes, I suppose that would be the answer, wouldn't it, Naomi?' The maternal voice prodded, asking for co-operation.

Naomi, whose energy seemed to have left her, could only acquiesce. She had no fight left now with which to do battle with the united front presented by her parents where Clare and her wonderful future were concerned.

'Good,' John Pemberton said jovially, rubbing his

hands and resuming his seat. 'Now, the wedding—since she's our daughter we must foot the bill, make the arrangements, invite the guests.'

'There's the reception, John,' murmured Sybil. 'Where's the best place to hold it?'

Fired into battle by her parents' bland assumption that she would sail unprotestingly through the marriage ceremony alongside a bridegroom whose only reason for marrying her was because he found her physically desirable, Naomi's temper ignited.

'All things considered,' she declared, 'I think it's my turn to have my say.' She twisted away from Gareth's encircling arm. He allowed her to go but reclaimed her a moment later. Her eyes caught fire at his action and she threw the heat at him like a flame-thrower trying to burn out an enemy.

Since all her tactics failed to shift him, she continued her tirade and it was her parents who recoiled. 'Let's get this straight,' she snatched her hand from Gareth who had taken it again and proceeded to use it to count on. 'There's going to be no reception, no guests apart from the nearest relatives. It's going to be a civil marriage. After all, as you would have it, I'm no untried virgin, am I? How could I be when, according to you, I've given birth to a baby?'

Sybil and John Pemberton looked at each other. They were cornered and knew it. John turned to his future son-in-law. 'Gareth,' the word was almost a plea, 'you must have your say now. Surely you agree there must be a reception? We have so many friends, and I'm sure you have, too.'

Naomi shot to her feet and cried to her parents, 'How can you ask Gareth, how can you? You know what you're doing to me. You can't deny it. I thought you loved me! I'm your daughter as well as Clare . . .' She rushed to the door, groping for it through a curtain of tears.

CHAPTER SIX

IN the hall, Naomi searched blindly for her coat. Two arms came possessively round her waist, turning her. With all her might she resisted, but Gareth would not let her go. He pulled her head down to his chest, stroking her hair while she sobbed against him.

Hearing a door open, Naomi pressed against him, seeking sanctuary from the two people she loved, yet who appeared to love her back so little they were willing to sacrifice her on the altar of their elder daughter's success.

The door closed again, and she sensed she was alone with Gareth. Lifting her head, she sought for a handkerchief, accepting his and using it. He lifted her face to his, taking back the handkerchief and drying her eyes.

'I don't want to go out for a drink,' she declared. 'There's nothing to celebrate.'

'I'm taking you out,' he insisted.

'I can't go anywhere now. I look terrible!'

'You look beautiful.' He spoke the words he plainly thought she wanted to hear. 'But if it makes you any happier, I'll wait until you do whatever you want to do to your face.' He turned her towards the stairs.

When Naomi came down, her mother was talking with something like urgency to Gareth. He was listening politely but impassively. Even though Naomi entered the room, the discussion went on. Her father appeared to be listening intently.

'You say you'll adopt the baby,' Sybil was saying. Gareth inclined his head. 'Is it really necessary, do you think? I mean, wouldn't it be better if Naomi just went on looking after her?'

Gareth gave one shake of the head. 'Completely unsatisfactory. I want a legal adoption.'

'Gareth,' John Pemberton cleared his throat, 'wouldn't it be better if you waited a bit? I mean, a few months of marriage, and you might find the whole process of adoption an unnecessary nuisance.'

Still Gareth shook his head. Husband and wife looked at each other, then both moved their attention to their younger daughter. Help us, they were silently urging her, it's in your interests that we're saying this.

Naomi remained obstinately silent. She knew the terms of her marriage to Gareth—his terms. They included adoption of the child he was convinced was hers.

'The father's permission would have to be given,' Gareth stated firmly, 'before I took a single step in that direction.'

'I—er—don't know that that would be necessary in law,' said John.

'Whether the law does or doesn't require it,' Gareth replied quietly, 'I do.'

Again, Naomi's parents' eyes met. Sybil Pemberton spoke for them both. 'We do understand, Gareth, my husband and I . . .' Inwardly her mother was quite unsure of her ground, Naomi knew that by the slightly bewildered expression.

Naomi was aware of how her mother would attempt to contact Brian because she had told her, but there was an embargo on telling Gareth—imposed by themselves. They could come clean about Becky's birth, they could tell him the truth if they wanted, she thought angrily, but because of the stage at which Clare's career was poised, they refused to do so.

'We'll do our best, Gareth,' her father promised, 'we'll do our best to get in touch with this young man we're talking about—even if I have to get an investigator on him.'

'I could do that myself, Mr Pemberton,' Gareth responded. 'If your wife has no success, I'll get someone on to this. Thanks, all the same.'

Naomi looked at Gareth, frowning. 'Your wife', he'd said, when before long her mother would be his mother-in-law.

Outside, as they made for the car, Naomi walked with unwilling feet. Gareth motioned her inside but she resisted, saying, 'I'd rather go home, Gareth.'

He caught at her words, his smile, in the light from the car's interior, faintly cynical. 'Home? This house is your home, isn't it?'

Naomi hoped the darkness would hide her quick surge of colour. She had called his home hers! Bending, she put herself into the passenger seat.

He got in beside her, switching on the car's external lights. 'Okay, I know what you mean. We're going out, all the same.'

The entrance to the ancient inn to which Gareth took her was through a narrow corridor and past the reception desk. Gareth helped her remove her coat and hung it with other people's near the swing doors which led to the large room which Naomi assumed was the bar.

It had been furnished with low, deeply upholstered chairs and settees. At Gareth's enquiry, Naomi named the drink she would like and chose a well-worn but comfortable chair.

Leaning back, she forced herself to unwind, cutting her thoughts free of the bitterness which her parents' refusal to tell Gareth the truth had caused. As Gareth leaned on his arm on the counter, she saw with a sting of pain how his attractiveness to her had, if that were possible, increased over the long months apart.

His leanness, the way he held his head, his brown

hair which just skimmed the edge of his tan polo sweater beneath his jacket, still touched off inside her the beginnings of the fire he had started two years before.

He had said she attracted him, too, so why had she taken such exception to his statement? The difference was love, she told herself. In that she had not wavered. He had lost his love for her in those two interminable years.

He was paying for the drinks, rooting in his pocket for the exact money. Naomi looked around, seeing couples seated close, talking animatedly as if they had not met for years. Yet what had she to say to Gareth, knowing his conviction that she had betrayed him?

He stood looking at her narrowly, put the drinks on the low table and pulled her upright with a suddenness that made her hit him. The contact was fleeting, but it was sufficient to set her pulses racing.

Gareth pushed her down on to the settee, gave her the drink he had bought her and lifted up his own. Taking care not to spill the liquid, he lowered himself beside her.

'Next time you try to put a chasm between us,' he threatened, 'I really will put you face down across here!' He indicated his knees.

She took a drink. 'You'd have a hard job getting me there,' she retorted, swallowing another mouthful.

'All the better.' His grey eyes glinted. 'I know what would follow.' He looked her over, dwelling on her legs. 'And that would be delightful. I haven't forgotten what it's like to lie beside you making love.'

'Don't talk to me about love,' she returned angrily, yet straining to speak quietly. 'Your *love* was so weak it couldn't last out for those two years we didn't see each other.'

'And you know why,' he muttered, his eyes at freezing point. He finished his drink and took away her nearly-empty glass. 'Come on, there's dancing through there. Let's join it.'

He caught her hand, pulling her. 'I don't want to dance with you,' she told him petulantly.

Gareth paused for a moment beneath a doorway topped by a heavy beam. It just cleared his head. Naomi stood beside him watching the dancers in the half-light. When Gareth swung her into his arms, she went without complaint, but her muscles tightened up on contact with the length of him.

'Naomi.' His voice drew her face upward, but she schooled her features to remain unresponsive. He pulled her nearer to him. 'I want to make love to you.' She pressed her lips together and shook her head. 'Tonight.'

'Don't be silly!'

'I've never been more serious.'

A shiver took hold, and he must have felt it by the way he eased her into a more intimate position against him. She turned her head away. 'I want to go.'

'Now you're being silly. The evening's just begun.'

Naomi looked around her. If I were Clare, she thought, I'd be in my element here, showing off my attractions and drawing attention to my acting talents by projecting my laughter and my jokes. But I'm not Clare, although I'm looking after her baby. Clare . . . Naomi faltered in her step and Gareth steadied her. Clare—*who could tell Gareth the truth!*

Her spirits soared. She would write to Clare and ask her to put the truth into writing. Then Gareth could not dispute it. It would be there in front of his eyes. In the morning, she would telephone her mother and ask for Clare's address. After that, it would all be straightforward.

There would be no need to find Brian since there would be no need for any adoption. The thought that she would soon be free of the burden of Gareth's condemnation had her mind singing.

She looked around her again. It was a swirl of colour and sound and she felt the tug of the rhythm. Then she shot a half-veiled glance in Gareth's direction. She found he had been watching her and he responded at once.

'Something's put a light in your eyes. Tell me.'

For a while, her body swayed and curved to match his sinuous movements. She knew she was inflaming him, and not only by the predatory look in his eyes. Everything about her held promise and that was how she wanted it to be. A question was swirling about in her mind like the colour and light around them, and it was vital that Gareth listened to her request.

'Come on, tell me,' he demanded, letting his hands slip down to rest on her hips.

The music stopped, but they did not move apart to await the next dance, as other couples did. He kept her there, hard against him, and for Naomi the rest of the world receded into infinity. Engulfed by the longing to yield to him, to give what he most desired of her, she clung to his shoulders, face uplifted to his. When his lips had descended, kissed and lifted, they left behind a smile.

'Tell me,' he urged again, and as the music came back to fill her head, she said, over its coaxing love theme,

'If I gave you a signed statement to read from my sister Clare that Becky was hers, would you believe me then, when I tell you Becky doesn't belong to me?'

'Ah, now I understand the reason for your change of mood.' There was silence between them for some while as they danced, his hands still on her hips, hers curved round his neck.

His lips nuzzled her ear and she shivered at the electric effect the action had on her nervous system. His lips told a different story when he lifted them and spoke.

'How would I know you hadn't connived with Clare to fool me, and that she was being sisterly by taking the blame on her shoulders?'

Naomi tore away from him. '*Her* shoulders? When I've taken all the burden on mine?'

'So you're being sisterly, is that what you're implying?'

'Yes, it is, and I am. And you can smile like that as much as you like, when you see Clare's letter telling you the truth, you'll have to believe it.'

'Okay, so I'll believe it. It obviously makes you happy if I say so.'

Naomi sparkled up at him. 'Yes, it makes me happy, and you needn't say it so condescendingly!'

Still they danced, and she felt drunk with the rhythm and the throbbing sounds, wondering if they came from the music or her heart. It was good to be in Gareth's arms again, feel his cheek against hers as she reached up to touch it.

'You look as if you've drunk too much,' he commented, holding her away to appraise her better, 'and you're behaving with a similar abandon.'

Taking his words as criticism, she tried to draw away, but he held her more tightly. 'Carry on,' he whispered, 'and I'll think you're back to being the girl I fell in love with.'

'And I'll think,' she answered with smiling impudence, 'you're the man I used to love two years ago.'

His face changed and an expression flitted over his features like a winter's day in midsummer. Naomi told herself she had imagined it, since a moment later he was smiling again.

When they arrived home, Eddie had fallen asleep in his chair. He awoke with a start. 'Good as gold, she's been, good as gold,' he muttered, rubbing a hand over his face.

Gareth went over to him, saying sympathetically, 'We came back early, but obviously not early enough. You go to bed, Father.'

Mr Gill gladly drew himself from the chair. Naomi glimpsed a look of Gareth in the older man's face. Strangely, it was of a transient bleakness, one she had momentarily caught and puzzled over in Gareth's eyes since his return.

As the door closed on him, Gareth dropped into a chair, his head back but his eyes alert. Naomi discovered that he was watching every movement she made. There was desire in his look and she remembered his words earlier that evening—*I want to make love to you tonight.*

When he spoke, his words were prosaic. 'Is this the first time you've left the baby in the evening?'

'I've left her before at weekends, when I visited my parents. Brian looked after her. Except for last time,' she recalled, 'when his mother came and stayed at the flat.'

'Now I wonder why you didn't take the child to your parents with you?' His gaze was narrow, inviting a reply.

Naomi refused to supply an answer. The whole situation was too involved, and until he really believed the truth, it would be pointless to try and explain.

For something to do, she looked at her watch. It was a nervous action and she was aware its jerkiness would not have escaped the notice of the man in the chair. He lifted his hand and beckoned, giving her a meaningful, underbrowed look.

'No, Gareth.' She had meant to sound firm, but the words turned themselves into a plea. 'Isn't it time we went to——' It was the worst thing she could have said!

'Bed.' He finished the question for her. 'Isn't that just what I was thinking?' He went across to her, pulling her back to the chair and on to his knee. With purpose in his eyes, he discarded his tie.

'No, Gareth,' she repeated, more firmly this time, following up her statement with a desperate effort to escape.

He held her by the arm and thigh. The touch of him was so electric she stopped at once and held her breath. He eased her back and his hand slid higher along her thigh, stroking, caressing, making her go cold with a shivering which in no time became a flare of fire.

Her arms lifted and curved around his neck, her lips parted as she murmured his name on a breath. His mouth covered hers, lifting and touching, and all the while he trailed his hand the length of her.

A curse escaped him as he found the tie neckline of her dress. Deft fingers soon demolished the barriers, and with the sureness of familiarity pushed a way through to settle in a possessive hold on the hardening swell of her breasts.

'Gareth, Gareth,' she whispered, holding his head in a frantic grasp and burrowing her forehead against the patch of chest hair revealed by unfastened buttons.

'Well, what is it to be,' he asked, his voice low, 'you'll come to my bed tonight?'

Naomi nodded without hesitation and held her breath as his mouth curved in a slow, anticipatory smile. There were a series of whimpers from overhead, which grew rapidly into a wail. Naomi's bright eyes, as they answered the brilliant urgency of his, dimmed to dullness.

'I'll have to go to her,' she stated flatly, pushing away from his warm, electrifying hold.

He held her tightly. 'She'll stop in a minute. Leave her.'

As if to maintain her right to summon her aunt to

her side, no matter what the time might be, Becky's protests grew louder.

'She'll disturb your father,' Naomi claimed, increasingly anxious to avoid the piercing scream the baby had perfected recently and which she had tried out with such success on her maternal grandfather.

Winning the battle for freedom this time, Naomi found herself out in the cold, standing in front of an angry man who watched her fumbling to fasten her blouse buttons. He did not offer to help, but made for the tray holding a couple of bottles, pouring himself a drink.

'Gareth,' Naomi looked with compassion at the stiffly furious back, 'I'm sorry.'

Her whisper of apology for a situation entirely beyond her control did not seem to have reached him. Upstairs, she faced a distressed baby who had thrown off her bedclothes. Picking her up, she walked her about, putting her back. Still Becky whimpered.

Changing her and taking her downstairs, Naomi made for the kitchen. She looked around wondering where to put the baby while she prepared a small feed of milk. There was not a single safe place to put her. Deciding to brave Gareth's ire, she took her to the sitting-room.

Gareth turned swiftly, then his anticipating eyes went cold at the sight of the fretful baby girl in Naomi's arms.

'Why have you brought the child in here?' he demanded, tossing down his drink and thumping the glass on to the tray.

'A warm drink might pacify her,' Naomi answered shortly, hiding her unhappiness at his lack of understanding. Lowering the baby on to a deep armchair and wrapping her tightly in a cot cover, she asked over her shoulder, 'Will you please make sure she stays there and doesn't roll on to the floor?'

Gareth motioned her irritably towards the door, implying that he wasn't so unfeeling as to let the baby injure herself.

Naomi returned quickly with the baby's bottle. As she entered, she saw Gareth studying the baby's face, while the baby-brown eyes gazed as unflinchingly back at him.

Were they, Naomi wondered, exchanging silent messages? Was it, on Gareth's part, a question-and-answer session—whose child are you? And was Becky answering, with her bold, unwavering stare, I'm my mother's child and no one else's?

He did not start with surprise, nor the faintest hint of guilt at being caught in his scrutiny. But it was with something near to distaste that he accepted the bottle thrust into his hand by Naomi, with a 'Would you hold that a moment, please?'

Naomi placed herself in the chair with Becky in her arms, then held up her hand for the bottle. On her face was a brilliant, challenging smile, but it was with irritation that Gareth gave her the bottle.

The level of the liquid lowered slowly and when Becky had had enough, she stopped. Smiling at the baby's knowledge of her own needs, Naomi lifted her gently to an upright position.

All the while, Gareth walked about the room, finally throwing himself into his chair. He closed his eyes as if he had a driving need to shut out the mother-child tableau opposite him, but there was plainly no rest in his body despite the late hour.

When Naomi started to untangle the baby's cover in order to wrap it around her, she felt impelled to look up. Gareth's eyes were on her. Their greyness had deepened almost to black and she heard herself whisper hoarsely,

'What's wrong?' He must have caught the words over Becky's baby-sounds.

'Wrong?' He wrenched himself from the chair. 'Don't you know?' He towered over her. 'Do you really not know? Don't you realise how it's driving me crazy seeing you sitting there loving—yes, loving that child?'

Naomi shook her head hopelessly but responded, 'Yes, I love her, just as I love all children.'

'And all men?'

The cutting remark made her flinch and close her eyes. She found herself burying her face in the baby's soft clothing for any scrap of comfort they might give her.

Having inflicted his wound, Gareth walked about again, coming to a stop once more in front of her. 'If that child were ours—*ours*, I'd give you the world . . .' His voice tailed off and he dropped back into the chair as if fatigue and hopelessness had caught up with him, too.

He had hurt her feelings so deeply, Naomi was beyond caring about his. 'For the use of my body?' she hurled at him.

He sat forward, gripping the chair arms, his face white with rage. 'Get out,' he snarled, 'and take that *precious, beloved* child of yours with you!'

Tears rose, but Naomi hid them by obeying his directive. She gathered the now-sleeping baby close and walked slowly from the room. After the evening they had spent together and his lovemaking afterwards, she wanted to sob her heart out of her body.

Climbing the stairs, she placed Becky in the carrycot, covered the still-sleeping form and crept out. She would clear the baby's bottle and other things from the sitting-room in the morning.

Daylight came too soon for Naomi. The hours she had slept had been short and disturbed. Half of her had wondered whether Gareth would keep his promise and come to her that night, the other half knew how disastrous such a coming-together would be.

He had not appeared. She had relaxed slowly and, she had truthfully to admit, disappointedly into formless and frightening dreams which, in the end, had bordered on nightmares.

Dressing and washing, she wondered if Becky had woken yet. There was no sound from the other closed doors. She discovered that the baby was still sleeping soundly, probably making up for the lost time in the night.

Gareth was at the breakfast table. As Naomi entered, he pushed aside the plate from which he appeared to have eaten a poached egg on toast. After a brief glance at her pale face and heavy eyes, he immersed himself in the Sunday newspaper.

Naomi followed his example and cooked an egg for herself. Halfway through eating it, she sighed and pushed the remainder aside, pouring herself coffee from the pot which he had made.

Turning the large news sheets and folding them, he looked across the table. 'Okay, I'll make the remark I'm supposed to make. You look tired. Why?' Hating his sarcastic tone, she did not answer. He smoothed the folds from the pages. When he continued, she did not expect sympathy, having seen the twist to his lips. 'After my stated intention of taking you to my bed, you probably lay awake half the night waiting for me.'

Again, Naomi forced her tongue to remain still. He would not provoke her!

'Pity if you did,' he hung an arm over the back of his chair, 'because after your acid remarks, I stopped fancying you. Also, there's nothing like seeing one's fiancée hugging the so-called love child she had by another man to cool one's passion.'

'Look, Gareth,' she answered, her tone intense, 'I can prove to you Becky isn't mine.'

'Don't go over that again. So produce the letter from your sister swearing the baby's hers, then I'll rethink our relationship. Maybe you'll even reawaken my dormant feelings for you.' He pushed back his chair. 'Much more,' she could see the flash of anger in his eyes, 'and you'll give them the kiss of death. Then out you go, child and all!'

'If it were in my power,' her voice was shaking now, 'I'd up and leave right now.'

He gave her a reducing glance. 'If you want me for anything, I'll be in one of my two rooms, working. My father will probably be down soon.'

Naomi nodded, rose and followed Gareth out, shadowing him as he climbed the stairs. Partway up, he stopped and turned irritably. 'What do you want?'

'Becky, to feed her.'

At the top, he watched her go to the door of the smaller bedroom. Something made her glance back. When she saw his stare of contempt, her heart twisted in agony.

Eddie Gill appeared in the kitchen while Naomi was spooning baby cereal into Becky's mouth. Naomi smiled 'good morning' and Becky gave him her usual stare. Strange, she thought, how she did not scream at this man as she had at her grandfather. She allowed herself a small smile at the irony.

'Can I cook you anything, Mr Gill?' Naomi asked.

'No, no, you stay where you are, dear. You've got enough on your hands. I'll clear a few of these things and get myself something. Heaven knows, I've had enough practice over the past years.'

He spoke with a muted bitterness, probably without even being conscious of it. 'I'm off today—did Gareth tell you? I won't stay for the wedding, dear. He couldn't give me a date, so I'll not hang around your feet any longer. My lady's waiting for me. Her name's Constance, but I call her Connie.' He busied himself with stacking dishes in the sink. 'Constant's something she will be, I know it without being told. Somehow, you know these things deep down, don't you?'

It took Naomi a few minutes to drag her mind away from the son's apparent lack of his father's deep feelings on the subject before she could answer with a smile,

'Not being a man, Mr Gill, I wouldn't know.'

He was grilling himself bacon and sausage and did not look round. 'But a woman knows it, too, doesn't she? Can't she sense which man will be faithful to her and which won't?' He half turned his head. 'Don't you know by now that Gareth wouldn't let you down, ever, and that, come what may, he'll stick by you?'

Come what may . . . They were the vital words and she guessed Mr Gill had known it, since she had not missed his glance at the baby in her arms.

Later, Gareth came down to drive his father to the railway station. Mr Gill kissed Naomi fondly on both cheeks. 'Cheer up, dear,' he encouraged. 'Gareth'll stand by you, I told you that.'

The man in question had walked impatiently to the car.

'Mr Gill,' Naomi held his sleeve, 'please believe me when I say Becky isn't mine. She's my sister's baby.'

He stared at the slim young hand as it rested on his sleeve. Then he patted it. 'Don't worry about it, Naomi dear. It's only natural you should want to start your married life free of any guilt feelings.'

Naomi removed her hand. 'So you still don't believe me!'

He started to speak, changed his mind and declared, 'Dear me, I'll miss that train if I'm not careful. All the best, Naomi dear. One day I'll bring my Connie to meet you. She's a wonderful lady.'

Naomi watched his tall, solid figure, shoulders

slightly bent, walk towards the car in which his son was waiting.

As they went down the drive, she hurried back into the house, seized a scrap of paper and wrote on it, 'Will clear all the mess when I get back, Naomi.'

Running a comb through her hair, she gave her casually-dressed reflection scant attention. She ran down to the patio area outside the sitting-room windows and scooped Becky out of the carrycot. Pausing, she put her back and lifted the cot section from the frame and walked with her to Brian's car.

A few minutes later she was making for her parents' house. Since it was a Sunday morning, she knew her father would be pottering in the garden. For the first time, she did not care. By the only means she knew, she was on her way to clearing her name.

It was the front garden on which John Pemberton had decided to work. When he saw his younger daughter swing into the wide drive in a battered and ancient car, he stopped digging to stare. The moment she slammed out of the driving seat and swung open the rear passenger door, lifting out the carrycot, he flung his fork in the earth and shouted,

'If I've told you once, I've told you a dozen times, I won't have Clare's illegal little brat in my house—and that's putting it very politely!'

Giving her father a brilliant smile, she continued locking the car doors, having lowered Becky's carrycot to the ground. 'I could say many things in answer to that, Dad, but——' another grin, 'I won't.'

He strode across the grass, mud clinging to his boots, white hair disordered by the breeze. 'Did you hear what I——'

A full-bodied shriek from the direction of the ground drowned the rest of the sentence and seemingly threw a bomb amongst his thoughts. Looking frankly bewildered, and, Naomi saw with amusement, somewhat battle-scarred, her father brought up his hands to protect his ears. With a wide smile, Naomi went on her way. Becky had, for the second time, vanquished her grandfather.

Sybil greeted her daughter and her elder daughter's daughter with delight. 'Coffee, Naomi. You must have a cup. It's perking in the kitchen.' She peered into the carrycot. 'Oh, you little darling! You're so like your mother, it's unbelievable.' She held out her arms to the fast-growing bundle with a cherubic face and restlessly-moving arms and legs.

'In a few minutes, Mum,' Naomi replied firmly. 'First, I want you to tell me something. Clare's address—I want to write to her. I won't phone, I won't call her, I'll just write.'

Sybil was shaking her head. 'I daren't, dear. She's getting on so well now,' sinking into a chair, 'what with being the leading lady, not to mention those offers she's had from London.'

'All I want to do is write to her,' Naomi repeated, finding a seat on the couch. 'Look, Mum, I want to clear my name with Gareth. Isn't that just as important to you as Clare's career?'

'Yes, yes, of course it is. You sound jealous, Naomi, but honestly, there's no need, you know. We love you just as much as we love——'

'I'm not jealous, Mother!' Naomi drew in her breath. 'All I want—and it would make me very happy to have it—is Clare's address.'

'Where's that coffee you called me in to have?'

No, Naomi thought with dismay, now my father's come in, my mother won't dare to tell me where Clare lives.

'I'm so sorry, John,' Sybil hurried to the kitchen, 'I forgot all about it.'

John Pemberton tutted, took a step inside, then caught sight of the carrycot which had been placed on a low table. Warily, he eyed it, looked at his daughter and said, 'I wish you hadn't brought——'

A high-pitched and indignant wail came from the cot's depths. Without realising it, John Pemberton had put himself into the line of vision of the baby within.

Moving quickly, he stepped back. 'Why doesn't she like me?' he asked with a touch of the spurned little boy. 'After all, I am her grandfather!'

The ironic twist of events so amused Naomi, she burst into laughter. Her father looked deeply discomfited. 'At least she notices you,' Naomi assured him, and laughed again at her father's changed expression. Her words appeared to have put straight his pride which had been knocked askew by his curiously knowing granddaughter.

On impulse, she turned to the carrycot, scooped up the occupant and lowered her into her astonished grandfather's arms. Both were taken so much by surprise, each was speechless. A creased and ruddy-complexioned face looked down into a smooth and rose-cheeked replica of his elder daughter.

Inquisitive, untried light brown eyes gazed wonderingly into deeper brown, nonplussed and oddly uncertain ones. Naomi watched as neither made a sound. Then a faint but clearly perceptible smile curved the tiny, rosebud lips. Older ones, with life-created creases raying from them, smiled back. Naomi realised with delight that her father was holding his breath. He was reacting with wonder and unexpressed pleasure to his granddaughter's very artful, totally feminine overtures.

Naomi found her mother standing wide-eyed, tray in hands, at the door. She, too, it seemed, was unable to speak. Then Naomi acted lest the spell was broken.

Disengaging Becky from her grandfather's arms, she placed her back in the carrycot. Her father, without a word, seized a cup of coffee from the tray and retreated to drink his elsewhere. Sybil lowered the tray to the table, began to comment, but stopped at once on seeing her daughter's finger being raised to her lips.

There was a prolonged silence as mother and daughter silently considered the consequences of the turnaround in the impossible situation which had prevailed until now.

Finishing her coffee, Naomi said, 'Clare's address—please, Mum.'

Sybil nodded, put her coffee aside and searched secretively inside a bureau, having first unlocked it. Relocking it, she carried an address book across to her daughter, provided her with a pencil and paper and read out the address.

After a few moments of writing, Naomi sighed with relief. She had just been given the key to the opening of the secret cave in which Gareth had locked away his love for her.

CHAPTER SEVEN

GARETH found her that evening seated, sealed envelope in hand, on the settee in the living-room. When he opened the door, she was staring unseeingly into the darker corners of the room.

Naomi did not raise her eyes when he entered. In fact, she showed no signs of realisation that she was not still alone. Her future life remained uncertain, even though she had rejoiced earlier that it would not be long before Gareth learned the truth from Clare.

A lowness of spirits had descended on her, and she knew exactly from which source it had originated—the man who had that moment come in. I want more, much more than just his ring and his name, she thought; I want his love. All this time, she had thought—had been certain—it still existed. Now she wondered just how much she was fooling herself.

He stood where he was for so long, she found her eyes lifting involuntarily to discover why. As their glances met, he moved his from her to the television set, then back to her.

'I thought you were watching that,' he remarked.

Naomi shook her head. 'I turned it off—I couldn't concentrate.'

'Too many things on your mind?'

Naomi glanced up, unsure as to whether he had spoken with sympathy. Seeing his smiling mockery, she knew he had not.

'That letter you've written,' he indicated the envelope in her hands, 'is the answer to it going to clear the pathway into the golden sunset for the two of us?'

'I hate your cynicism,' she spat back. 'Actually, as I sit here,' her eyebrows acquired, she hoped, a touch of disdain as she raised them at him, 'I'm wondering if there's really any need to accept you as part of my life, after all.' She closed her eyes, wondering if she would ever forgive herself for the lie.

He was in front of her in a few strides. 'Superior little bitch! I'll show you how much you *need* me!' The letter was snatched from her and thrown aside, landing on an armchair.

There had been no chance to protest since he had twisted her round to lie across him. He pulled off her sandals and threw them, one by one, across the room.

Her ribbed cotton sweater was being tugged over her head, stifling her cries to him to 'stop doing this to me'. Her head found a hard resting place on the arm of the settee, but she could not lift it. He had put an arm under her chin, holding it down. Her thrashing legs were stilled in a similar manner, leaving the way free for his mouth to play havoc with her senses.

His lips closed over the enlarged pink tips of her breasts, teasing them with his teeth and tongue until she writhed beneath his hold. Removing his gripping fingers from her ankles, he loosened her skirt waistband and pushed it down, stroking her waist and stomach, making the muscles tauten until she could scarcely bear the longing to have him take her wholly.

Lifting his head, he smiled with a hard pleasure at her pleading, brilliant eyes. 'Tell me you need me,' he commanded, 'tell me you can't live without me.'

Her throat was dry and she shook her head. His fingers found more sensitive places, feathering them with tantalising touches until she cried out loud the words he had ordered her to say.

At last, he removed his imprisoning elbow and Naomi lifted herself to grasp his arms, still covered by his rolled-up shirt sleeves. His chest was bared and as her arms wound around him, she felt with increasing excitement the abrasive rub of his chest hair against her soft flesh.

'Oh, Gareth, Gareth,' she whispered, her head drooping to rest on the hard hollow beneath his neck, 'I love you so, I love you. If you loved me in the same way it would transcend everything, even the awful things you think I've done since you went away . . .'

He was already pushing her from him when the telephone rang.

Standing now, staring down at him as he continued to sit, knees apart, shirt open, fingers spread wide on his thighs, she felt her lip tremble. 'It's true what I've just said,' she insisted, 'it's true!'

A mocking eyebrow rose as he looked her over in her half-dressed, dishevelled state. 'Shouldn't you answer that thing before it wakes the child?'

Hating his sardonic smile, she swung from him to the door, snatching a jacket from the coats cupboard and pulling it on.

'Naomi dear?' It was her mother. 'I'm sorry to ring you so late. I hope I didn't drag you out of bed?'

Naomi answered wearily that no, she wasn't in bed. Gareth came from the sitting-room, took up a jacket and went out. As the front door banged shut, Naomi felt a distressing sense of loss.

'Well, I thought you'd like to know,' her mother went on 'that I managed to contact Clare. She always sleeps late on Sundays to catch up on her rest, but I expect you understand that? I mean, she works so hard all week.' Naomi decided that a reply was neither necessary nor expected. 'Well, I asked her if she knew her young man Brian's address, but she said she didn't, not now. His job took him around and his digs keep changing.'

'You didn't tell her why I wanted to speak to Brian,

did you, Mother? I mean, it's Brian who's so fond of Becky.'

'No, I didn't tell her.' Naomi could not suppress a relieved sigh. 'But I think you're being unfair to your sister, dear. She loves her baby, I'm sure she does.'

Naomi's sigh this time was long-suffering. 'So why did she leave her in the crucial first few months of life?'

'Well, I—I mean, there was——' Naomi listened patiently to her mother's verbal flounderings. 'She knew you were there, didn't she?' Sybil produced the slightly outrageous statement with relief.

'Oh, Mother!' Naomi reproached, almost crumpling under the weight of resentment and ingratitude of the one person in the world who should surely have seen her point of view.

'Well, there you are. I've done my best, dear. It seems to me it's going to be very difficult to contact Brian.'

'All the same, he'll have to be contacted somehow.'

'Yes, dear.' Had mother heard her daughter's firmness, her inflexibility of purpose?

There was a small silence. 'Well,' Naomi filled in at last, 'thank you for trying.'

'That's all right.' Sybil responded brightly. 'Look after yourself, won't you, dear?'

'And Becky,' Naomi added for her, and put down the phone.

Returning to the sitting-room, Naomi found her clothes scattered round the room and put them on tiredly. Curling up on the settee, she rested her head on a cushion. When she had been a child, she had cuddled a corner of her pillow. She had imagined it to be her mother to whom she was clinging for the comfort and security she had assumed, in her innocence, that all mothers gave their young.

Idly, she wondered why she had thought this,

because she now knew it wasn't true. 'My mother's got plenty of love and comfort to give,' she thought aloud, 'but she gives it to Clare, not to me. Ah well,' she rubbed her cheek against the cushion, 'it's a good thing I didn't realise it in those days. I'm older and stronger now. I can take it.'

Her thoughts grew hazy and sleep took over.

Startled into semi-wakefulness, Naomi found that someone was beside her. The settee must have been too small to take them both, for the man who was with her was holding her surprisingly closely.

'Gareth?' she muttered sleepily. 'Where have you been?'

'To post your letter. You wanted it posted, didn't you?'

She found herself nodding against soft chest hairs. 'It won't go out tonight, though. No collection on Sundays.'

'At least it's on its way.'

'Yes, yes, it is.' Her murky brain tried to solve the puzzle of why Gareth should be as concerned as she was about the letter, but its powers of reasoning were overtaken again by sleep.

In the morning, when she awoke, she was on her own bed, partly-dressed and covered by a quilt. The clothes that were missing, she discovered, were her skirt and top. The fact that it could only have been Gareth who had removed them made her feel warm. He must have been considerate and gentle in his actions. The thought of his being so with her made her heartbeats quicken. Was his attitude towards her softening at last?

It was not until the midday meal that she saw him. He came down when she called upstairs that the food was on the table. Before taking his seat in the dining-room, he came round the table and took her in his arms. If her joy at his actions showed on her uplifted face, she did not care.

His mouth took its time over the kiss and even wanted a second after the first had ended. 'Thank you,' she whispered, 'for putting me to bed.'

He smiled, brushed her lips with his again and went back round the table. 'It was as much as I could do not to join you there.'

Naomi took up her knife and fork. 'I wish——' She closed her lips, stealing a look at Gareth. He smiled, plainly having guessed the subject of her wish.

'If my bodily appetite weren't at this moment so strong that it even outdoes my carnal impulses, I'd make your wish come true.'

Eating as she was, there was nothing she could do to hide the colour that swept her cheeks. As the meal progressed, Gareth told her about his experiences on the dig and how he was enjoying writing about them in the form of a long report.

'It will have to be completed before the new academic session,' he told her. 'Later on, I might need help.'

They were on to coffee now.

'You mean from one of your brainy archaeological colleagues?'

'I mean from that brainy administrative assistant who used to work in the same university department as I did.' He drank a mouthful of coffee then rubbed the back of his head in a seemingly puzzled gesture. 'Didn't I propose marriage to her once?'

Naomi smiled into her own empty cup. 'Did you? I'm not sure I remember that.' Then she looked at the ring on her hand. 'Perhaps you're right. Isn't that piece of jewellery yours? Or,' her eyes sparkled with provocation, 'have I got you mixed up with another man?'

He shoved back his chair, gripping it. 'You

impudent little baggage! If you talk about "another man" to me, I'll put you in your place and keep you there all night until you shout for mercy!'

Laughing at the annoyance she had aroused in him, she put his ring to her lips. He started round the table, only to be halted in his tracks by a cry from overhead.

In a moment, his good humour had passed and he uttered a forceful expletive. It was while Naomi was attending to Becky's many needs that he came down the stairs wearing his jacket and clinking his car keys.

He stood for a few silent seconds watching Naomi manage the increasingly demanding child, then he said shortly, 'I'm driving into the town. There are a few books I need to consult at the public library.'

She nodded, trying a smile on him, hoping to rekindle his happier mood. There was no answering smile on his blank face. He went out and Naomi heard the angry revving of his car. She sighed deeply and Becky, feeling it, lifted a hand to touch Naomi's cheek. Naomi hugged her closely.

About mid-afternoon, Naomi started to weary for Gareth's return. When Becky awoke from her rest, Naomi placed a pillow behind her head and shoulders so that she could see more of the world around her.

The carrycot was on the floor and Naomi knelt beside it, studying the baby. She was five and a half months old now. Her dark hair was soft and fluffed into tiny curls. Naomi wondered how any woman, let alone her own mother, could walk off and leave such a beautiful child.

She leant forward and tickled the baby's middle. Becky made gurgling noises and Naomi chuckled, saying, 'You're a cuddly bundle, do you know that?'

'Remember she's mine, not yours.'

The words from the doorway made Naomi swing round, her breath held in fear. She knew the colour had left her cheeks because they had turned so cold.

'Clare!' Naomi frowned. 'You couldn't have got my letter yet.'

The dark-haired young woman might have been Naomi's twin, except that her two extra years were evident in subtle ways, like the more worldly look in her eyes, the greater maturity of her figure. She had other things, too, that Naomi could not have possessed, like the veneer of sophistication put there by her theatrical ambition and its fulfilment.

Her pale blue summerweight jacket and matching skirt must, Naomi decided, rising from her kneeling position, have borne Manchester's equivalent of a Bond Street label. Her sister's hair, longer than her own, had been expertly fashioned.

Peeling off her fine leather gloves—they matched perfectly the colour of the suit—Clare walked slowly, stage-style, towards the carrycot. *Gloves,* Naomi thought. Who is she out to impress? Her parents, her sister—or herself?

'I haven't had any letter from you.' She stood beside the carrycot, eyes averted from its occupant. 'Why do you think I came? Mother phoned me, didn't she, saying you wanted Brian's address. She made out your case to be so pitiful, I thought I'd find you prostrate with a nervous breakdown or something.'

'A mother, even a substitute one, can't allow herself to be ill, either mentally or physically. You'll learn that one day, when you come tumbling off your career ladder and take responsibility for what you've done.'

'Why should I ever do that when you're doing such an excellent job with my child?'

'Yours! I'm glad you acknowledge her as such.' Naomi turned and lifted Becky out and placed her unceremoniously in her mother's arms.

Naomi had expected the now-familiar scream, but after a few moments of protest, Becky quietened. She turned her large eyes on to the face above her, a face that was so like her aunt's she might, in her dazed little mind, have mistaken Clare's identity.

Then Clare spoke, and the voice difference was so great no child attuned as finely as Becky's ears were to differences in sound could make the mistake that Clare and Naomi were the same person.

'You little darling,' Clare admired, 'you're going to be a real beauty. Brian and I did well, didn't we, Becky?'

'Coffee?' Naomi asked in a flat voice. Clare lifted her head, nodding. Naomi knew from their brilliant but only half-aware expression, that this time Clare was not acting.

Returning with the coffee, she found Clare talking softly to a listening, fascinated baby. The small hand was grasping the chunky beads around Clare's throat. Baby sounds, meaning pleasure, were coming from her.

Seeing her sister with a tray took the softly maternal expression from Clare's face and the veneer was back. Clare turned on the helpless little woman act and held out the baby. 'You can have her back now.'

'Don't be stupid, Clare,' Naomi reproached. 'I've got the tray, haven't I? There's the carrycot. You can put her back.'

The dizzily feminine bewilderment was put aside like a stage outfit. With a sureness of purpose, Clare replaced her cooing baby in the carrycot, adjusting the pillow. The moment she took her seat again, the pose of rejection of all things maternal returned.

'Where's the man who's going to make an honest woman of you?' Clare took some coffee from her sister's outstretched hand.

'If you mean Gareth, he's gone to the library to consult reference books.' Naomi drank her own coffee, sitting in the chair nearest to Becky. 'And if you take that attitude to me, Clare, I'll bundle the baby into

Brian's car, give you his keys, and force you to accept your little error back into your life!'

Clare continued to drink, seeming to have nothing to say.

'What's more,' her sister went on, 'I don't care a damn if the possession of a baby outside wedlock does ruin your acting career. Up to now, you've had it easy.'

The mask had fallen from Clare's face. 'Easy? I've worked my guts out getting to the top! In rep, where I've been since I left Brian, I've made it to the leading part. I'm about to clinch a deal with a London-based theatrical agency for the star part in a London musical. I've fought hard, do you understand?'

'So you've fought hard and worked hard—for yourself and your self-glorification. So have I worked hard—for your child. I gave up my job to care for her. I've lost my chance of a life of happiness because of your selfishness!'

'What do you mean?' Clare was leaning forward now. 'Gareth's going to marry you, isn't he, despite the baby?'

'He hates me for what he thinks I've done.'

'Haven't you told him Becky's mine?'

'I've lost count of how many times. He still doesn't believe me. We're so alike, you and I, the baby looks like both of us. He sees me in her, not you.' Naomi stood up, staring down at her sister. 'Clare, I want you to tell him the truth. That's what my letter says. I want you to answer it and put the truth into writing so that he can read it in black and white. I want you to tell him Becky's not my baby, she's yours.'

CHAPTER EIGHT

THERE was a key in the front door and it was opening. The two sisters froze, staring at each other. Clare was the first to come to terms with the situation.

Gareth came in and Naomi's heart turned over at the sight of him. His dark green jacket was unzipped, showing his brown, open-necked shirt. Fawn cords encased his legs and thighs, tightening to creases across his hips. A brown leather belt showed up the leanness of his waist.

All this Clare took in at a glance, her eyes distinctly appreciative.

'Gareth!' she exlaimed, in her role-playing voice. 'Growing older has definitely given you a certain something. My little sister's knight in shining armour! He always was, wasn't he, Naomi?' Gareth removed his jacket, throwing it towards a chair and missing. Clare watched every move he made. 'I wish you were mine,' she added, her eyes still on him as he threw himself into the chair his jacket had missed.

His answer to her provocative comment was a lift of his eyebrows. His glance lingered on her, frankly admiring. When it shifted to his fiancé, a shutter came down on his thoughts.

'Would you like some coffee?' Naomi asked him, her voice as expressionless as his face. 'Or tea?'

'Tea, but I'll make it.' His eyes returned to Clare who visibly preened herself under his contemplation.

Naomi cursed herself for having dressed so carelessly that morning. She had not had a single moment in which to look at her own reflection, let alone change out of her working blouse and cotton skirt.

All of her, from her untidy hair to the odd stain on her clothes, down to the broken-strapped sandals, bore the marks and smears of a young woman in charge of a growing baby.

Clare's baby, she thought rebelliously, my niece, not my daughter. She wished she could shout the fact aloud to the hard-headed, impenetrable man sitting across the room.

'Were you successful in your search for information?' she asked him, playing the interested fiancée.

'Not at the library. I had to make the journey to the University. There were books in my room and I thought they might help. In the end, Pam found what I wanted in the University library.'

Naomi frowned, jealousy at once niggling at her. 'Pam? Pam Hatton?' He nodded. 'The girl who was with you in York? And who answered the phone that day?' She could not add, in front of her predatory sister, The day you refused to talk to me. He nodded again. His lifted eyebrow asked silently, What concern of yours is it that she was there?

Becky, having grown tired of playing with the large coloured beads stretched across the carrycot, made attention-seeking noises.

'She's a beautiful child, Gareth, don't you think?' Clare was asking as Naomi's regard turned from Becky to her companions.

'Clare?' Naomi asked sharply. 'Will you tell Gareth——'

'How lucky he is,' her sister cut in smoothly, 'to have a wife-to-be who produces such beautiful children? Yes, I'll tell him. What kind do you want to go with Becky, Gareth? A son, or maybe another daughter? Whatever it is, you'll know one thing in advance—Naomi can certainly look after babies really well.'

'Clare!' Naomi cried, aghast at her sister's treachery. 'You know Becky's yours, yours and Brian's. Tell Gareth the truth. Be unselfish for once—tell him for my sake, for all I've done for you and Becky!'

Clare affected a deep frown. 'Connive with you, you mean?' She sounded sincerely horrified. 'Pretend you didn't live with Brian and look after his child?' There followed an accomplished pout. 'Shame on you, Naomi, to think you'd try to get me to join you in deceiving Gareth by hiding the truth from him!'

The man she mentioned tore himself from his chair, threw a firebrand of a look at Naomi and slammed from the room.

White-faced, Naomi stared at her sister. In a choked voice, she said, 'I'm asking you to leave.'

Was it guilt that made Clare's answering shrug such a defensive gesture? She stood up, peering into the carrycot. 'At least let me say goodbye to my lovely baby.'

'Leave this house, Clare. I don't ever want to see you again.' Naomi's tone was so firm she almost convinced herself there was no reservoir of tears gathering behind her eyes.

'You'll see me again, darling. In the glossies, the papers, on the telly. My name will be in lights outside the West End theatres.'

Clare was almost at the door.

'On my marriage to Gareth, he's going to adopt Becky,' Naomi said quietly. 'But he insists on having her father's permission first, which is why we must have Brian's address. Otherwise he'll put investigators on to finding him. You see,' the words were sweet-sour from a tear-tautened mouth, 'he thinks—always has—that I'm the baby's mother. So he wouldn't ask your permission, would he?'

Naomi did not see Gareth for the remainder of the evening. She ate a solitary evening meal, having attended to all Becky's needs and put her to bed.

Later, she heard Gareth descend the stairs, and her heart raced. At the slam of the front door, it slowed to normal. She had put on a tape of classical music, telling herself she had not done so in an effort to lure Gareth into the room.

Hearing his car drive away, she curled up on the settee and seized the cushion, holding it against her ribs. But it held no magical powers. In her childhood it might have comforted her. Now, she knew for certain that it would not take away the pain from an aching heart.

Gareth had not returned when she made for her bedroom. When she was halfway up the stairs, the telephone rang. She raced down, expecting to hear his voice, however sharp it might be, but her spirits sank when she heard a bright, young woman ask for 'Dr Gill.'

'I'm sorry, but he's out. No, I don't know where. Possibly his office at the University? No? You're there, but he isn't? Are you Pam Hatton? You are?' Naomi managed to sound cheerfully surprised. 'Sorry, Miss Hatton, but I can't help you. You could try again in the morning.'

Slowly she replaced the receiver. It was small consolation, but at least she knew he was not with that young woman. She would charm the reserve off any man. I wish I had her powers, Naomi thought, trudging upward as though the stairs were a summitless mountain.

Having taken a bath and slipped on her short nightdress, she nibbled her nails, wondering what to do. If she got into bed knowing Gareth hadn't returned, she was convinced she would stay awake listening for him. Taking up a book, she put on a silky dressing-gown and sat in the basket chair which occupied a corner of the room.

After every paragraph, her mind cut out and her

listening system switched on. It picked up a sound for which she was not prepared—a muffled cry from Becky's room. The book was put aside and, pushing her feet into mules, Naomi made for the source of the sound.

It took a few minutes to soothe the restless baby. Numerous pats on the back later, Naomi lowered her into the carrycot, covered her and left her sleeping.

Emerging from Becky's room, she swallowed a gasp as Gareth appeared at the top of the stairs. His humour was, if anything, worse than when he had left the house. He cast a bludgeoning look at Naomi, bouncing it off to the room behind her, including in its path the occupant of that room.

'Gareth—' Naomi was thrust aside by a remorseless arm. 'Pam Hatton phoned.'

He did not seem to hear. 'Get out of my way!'

The faint aroma of alcohol drifted in his wake. Naomi did not have to guess where he had spent the evening. He left his door ajar and Naomi, as she returned to her bedroom, heard the thud of his shoes and the throwing aside of discarded clothing.

As soundlessly as she could manage, she slipped inside her room and closed the door. Instinct told her not to attract her fiancé's attention.

Still she hesitated about going to bed. She knew it would be impossible to relax. Earlier, the cause had been his prolonged absence from the house. Now, it was because he had come back.

He had thudded into the bathroom. He emerged almost as loudly. Perhaps he would simmer down when the soporific effect of his bath had taken effect. She tried not to remind herself that sometimes a bath re-energised, taking away fatigue.

Since she could not spend the rest of the night walking aimlessly around, she slipped off her dressing-gown and hung it on the door. Turning out the main light and leaving on only the bedside lamp, she folded back the quilt.

With her knee on the bed, she watched unbelievingly as the door moved open. There was fear in her eyes as she raised them to Gareth's face. A barely suppressed anger had been honed to spear-points in his eyes.

They dropped from Naomi's face to rake the curving shape of her which, now that she was standing, she realised with dismay, showed clearly beneath her nightgown. Then his gaze lifted again and she felt impaled, a scream of anguish only just trapped in her throat.

'What's the matter?' she whispered, feeling her flesh drain of warmth.

He closed the door and locked it, standing guard with his arms folded and his long legs planted firmly apart. Beneath his short robe, he was bare to the waist, where only a pair of dark underpants covered him. Small beads of moisture were sprinkled across his forehead. Maybe he had showered instead of taking a bath, she reasoned, seeking for an ordinary, everyday happening in an effort to lessen her tension.

'The matter?' he repeated her question. 'You ask what's the matter?'

His rage was like a gathering storm, and she grew even colder in the swirling air currents preceding its unleashing. He wrenched himself from the door, moving across and towering over her faintly trembling form.

'So Clare would tell me the truth, would she?' he rasped. 'No, she would say, Becky's not Naomi's baby, she's mine. Is she hell!' He fastened a biting grasp around her upper arm and slammed her against him. 'Why don't *you* admit the truth, that you lived with your boy-friend and gave birth to his child?'

Naomi was silent, staring up at at him. He seemed a stranger, his jaw rigid, his mouth a livid line. This was not the man who had made passionate love to her two years ago. This was a frightening enemy, unforgiving and seeking only to punish—for what crime, she cried out inside, for taking on uncomplainingly the care and welfare of her sister's baby?

Her sense of justice cried out, too—for a chance to be expressed. Yet if she tried again to defend herself by denial, Gareth would believe her even less now than he had before.

His hands were pressurising their way over her shoulders and down her arms. Reaching her wrists, his palms slid to her thighs, then upwards towards her hips. As his hands moved, so the filmy gown went with them until, with an incensed tug, he pulled it over her head, kicking the gown aside.

He let his hands slide round to her rear, holding her against him and making her feel his need. Every nerve in her body was alive, her pulses throbbing. 'Lean back,' he commanded, 'lean back. I want to see the woman I'm going to marry.'

'You've seen me,' she told him, her voice wavering at his cold-bloodedness, the way a man would treat a one-night woman, 'don't you remember? That night we made love, before you went away.' Had she stirred his memories of those wonderful moments they had so intimately shared?

'I saw you—but through tinted spectacles, rose-coloured, like your body now. But the bloom has gone,' he added cruelly. 'And I was not the man who took it away.' He held her more closely still and her desires flared, catching the whole of her alight. 'Do as I say, lean back.'

Naomi stood stiffly, hands fisted at her sides. His mouth hit hers, forcing her back until she had to uncurl her fingers and cling to his muscled, hard shoulders.

Gareth smiled and his expression was all-male,

alight with potency and a hungry need. His lips claimed her provocative, piquant breasts and Naomi's responses thundered with her heartbeats. Small, pleading sounds came from her throat and she found she had no control over them.

'Remove my robe,' he ordered, and she did so as though mesmerised. He lifted her and fell with her on to the bed. A few moments later there was nothing to prevent her feeling the hard desire of him against her.

His hands pressed in her cheeks, forcing open her mouth, and his exploration of it was as thrusting and possessive as his taking over of her will-power had been. When she was nearly crazy with longing for him, she heard herself cry, 'Gareth, love me, love me, please!'

From somewhere came a low, triumphant laugh and he invaded her very essence, taking her to heights she had never known before, of pleasure and shared and limitless joy.

Waking in daylight, she found him watching her. There was a cover over them, but his bare shoulders were above it. His arm reached out and turned her on to her side, moving her across to him and entangling his legs with hers.

His hand lightly massaged her hip and thigh. 'My God, how do you do it?' The back of his other hand feathered her cheek. 'You look as innocent as the day you were born!'

Naomi did not answer, rubbing her fingers over his roughened upper lip.

'I'd meant to punish you, hurt you, thrash you,' he went on. 'But—' he shook his head as if the words he wanted were elusive, 'you touched a part of me that went beyond my wish for revenge and reached my reason.'

She gasped as his hand touched her breast softly,

caressing it with his eyes and his fingertips. 'What – what did your reason tell you?'

'That anyone as guileless as you seemed to be couldn't have gone to the lengths that you went to.'

'The lengths that I went to?' she took him up. 'No doubts, not even now?'

'None, since the witness you were relying on – your sister – to get you off the hook told the truth instead.'

'Her truth, Gareth.' Her hand clutched his, stilling its arousing movements as it found new places which sparked off her desire. 'Not my truth.'

The words she had just uttered seemed to scratch the wafer-thin layer that covered his anger. He removed his hand from her and swung out to stand beside the bed. The sight of him, strong and powerful, made her arms reach out. He gathered her wrists in one of his hands, lifted her to the bed's edge, then stopped, pushing her away.

He pulled on his robe. 'In two days' time, we're marrying.' He tied the belt. 'I've seen to all the preliminaries. Do you want family or friends to be there? If you do, I'll arrange a meal for after the ceremony.'

Naomi turned away from him, on to her side. He went to the door, bringing him back into her line of vision. 'No, thank you,' she answered, 'not since you're only marrying me because of your strong sense of duty. Not forgetting,' she flung after him, 'the most important reason of all – that you want my body so much you can't keep your hands off me. You said it,' as he made to come at her from the doorway, 'I didn't.'

The door slammed. Almost at once, a wail reached her. He had woken Becky and now she wouldn't stop yelling until her needs were attended to.

Life was so unfair, she thought, swinging her legs out of bed. It didn't even give her the chance to cry her sense of grievance and her distress out of her system.

Gareth had beaten her to the kitchen, Naomi discovered. The pine tray was missing, which probably meant that he had taken his breakfast upstairs to his room.

It made her sad to think that, after a night spent together, he did not have the inclination to share the breakfast table with her, too, continuing the intimacy, but on a different plane. Laughing together, she thought, as well as loving together. There had been no laughter since they had met again, only a gnawing bitterness which killed all spontaneity.

Washing the dishes, she turned to see Gareth bringing in his tray. He was dressed for going places, she noted with a sinking heart. His tasteful brown and fawn check jacket looked good with his tan rollnecked shirt. The suede elbow patches told her his destination was probably not a meeting with other academics, but his place of work.

His words confirmed her guess. 'I'm researching again today.'

'University or public library?'

'The former.'

Her back swung to him and she mopped the dishes. 'You wouldn't be going just to get away from me?'

There was a short silence. 'Now, if ever there was an invitation . . .' he remarked, his voice revealing amusement. 'But I'm not taking it. Once I got my hands on you –'

'You wouldn't be able to get them off.' She turned, placing her back to the sink. 'Well, in future, you can keep them entirely and completely to yourself. Do you understand?' Her eyes blazed defiance, but he was moved to further amusement.

Hands slid into unbuttoned patch pockets. 'Do you

really think a little word like "no" would put me off? In fact . . .' he went towards her, his unspoken intention obvious in his half-smile and underbrowed look. He gripped her shoulders and jerked her close. There was an angry cry from the other room where Becky was meant to be sleeping.

Gareth thrust her away disgustedly. 'Has that child got her timing right! How more like her mother can she get?'

Naomi stared at him. Had he guessed the truth after all? Her spirits soared and exploded with the brilliance of fireworks. When he remarked, 'Will she develop your warped idea of the truth, too?' they fell in a curve and faded into blackness.

He was gone all day. To fill in the time, Naomi cleaned the place through, then took Becky shopping. One look at her clothes as they hung on the rail had reminded her how much she had neglected herself over the past few months. There was not a single thing she could wear to the wedding. It was with a shock that she realised it would be *her* wedding, not someone else's.

Having drawn on her savings instead of using the money which Gareth had given her for her own and Becky's keep, Naomi pushed the carrycot on its frame into the lift of one of the towns' department stores.

Keeping Becky near, she went from rail to rail in search of the most appropriate outfit. It mustn't be dark, she reasoned, nor white, nor floral. Smilingly she had refused the assistant's offer of help. She had no wish to reveal that the dress for which she was searching was intended for her wedding. Since Becky was so obviously with her, it would have been too embarrassing to bear the woman assistant's nodding but knowing acquiescence.

The dress she bought was of the palest lilac. Its cut was expensively good, its style simplicity itself, and she added white accessories. Piling her parcels into the car's boot and lifting Becky on to the rear seat, securing the carrycot with the harness, Naomi felt pleased with her purchases.

At least I won't let Gareth down, she reflected, driving home. In my dress I'll be all he expects of a bride, even if, in his eyes, my moral behaviour has gone badly wrong. Still the injustice of it all tightened her lips and produced an ache around her heart.

Gareth returned as she was clearing away her evening meal. 'I didn't cook for you,' she told him. 'If you'd called me, I'd have kept something, but you didn't, so I didn't bother. Perhaps,' her wide eyes challenged, 'you're not only working in the past, but living in it, too, which is why you may not know the telephone's been invented.'

He drew in his breath and gave a good imitation of a wince. 'Acid corrodes,' he commented, removing his jacket and answering her reluctant smile with a broad one of his own.

'If someone gave me a truth drug, whatever that may be, I expect you still wouldn't believe me.'

He glanced upwards, indicating Becky's bedroom, then at the few toys scattered around. 'Actions speak louder than words, as they say.'

'You're so trite,' she turned on him, 'so pigheaded!'

He frowned, then annoyed her more by staying silent.

'Your work over the past two years has been piecing tiny fragments together, hasn't it? Pieces of the past? Can't you use those abilities on everything I've told you, plus what you surely must have observed for yourself, since you came back?'

He sat in a dining chair, resting his elbows on the table and clasping his hands. His shoulders stooped a little, his whole appearance spoke of weariness. Naomi's heart went out to him, wanting with all her heart to hold his head against her breasts where it had rested in the night.

'There's one incontrovertible bit of evidence in all this.' He was studying his thumbs, comparing their lengths. 'Your sister's.'

Naomi took a deep breath, closed her lips and contained her wrath. Pushing the dishes through the serving hatch, she swept into the kitchen. Calling through it from there, she asked, 'You didn't say if you wanted any food.'

'I've eaten.'

She did not know what impulse made her ask, 'With Pam Hatton, I suppose?' At once, she cursed herself.

He rose, disappeared momentarily, then reappeared to lean against the kitchen door. 'As a matter of fact, I did. We found a cosy little wine bar and had sandwiches and a few drinks.'

Naomi's hands took over the battle, banging crockery into the sink. Again, she became annoyed with herself, the more so when he commented, 'It sounds like you're jealous. I'm glad. Maybe it gives you a very small insight into how I've been feeling where you're concerned.'

She turned to face him. 'Taking another woman for a meal was just another way of punishing me, was it? Your sentiments, as spoken by you last night.'

He cut across her challenge. 'Have you managed to contact your boy-friend?'

For a moment she wondered who he was talking about – what boy-friend? Turning back to the dishes, she said, 'You mean Brian, I suppose. No.'

'I should be glad if you'd try a bit harder,' he answered quietly. 'There's no way I'll adopt your child without his consent.'

'Surely you don't need it in law?'

'I don't care what the law says, in this case I'm making my own.'

Naomi dried her hands and removed her apron. Gareth was watching her all the time. His hands were in his pockets. Was he keeping them there to stop himself from touching her?

Having finished in the kitchen, she needed to pass him in order to gain entrance to the other room. 'Excuse me, please.' Her eyes lifted, met the glint in his and felt even more strongly the need to escape.

He did not move. His mouth was curving and, in desperation, she began to push past him. The contact seemed to fire him to action. His hands whipped free and wrapped around her. Moving from one foot to the other, he rocked her with him. Her arms were forced to curl around him, too.

'Kiss me,' he demanded.

Assuming disdain, she turned her head away.

'Kiss me,' he repeated, 'or I'll bed you here and now. Or,' he whispered in her ear, 'isn't that a threat?'

Naomi smiled. The light in his eyes was so brilliant, she felt blinded. Her love for him took over and she stood on tiptoe, rooting around for his mouth with her own. He did not make it easy for her, holding himself just out of reach.

Succeeding at last, she kissed him, then stopped, annoyed by his refusal to co-operate. Laughing, he took the situation over, holding her against him and probing her mouth until she felt as though her bones were melting within her.

He left her breathless and bright-eyed. As she walked towards the living-room, she turned to find him following her and discovering a frown on his face. Not wishing to disturb the good relations between them, she decided not to ask him what was wrong.

He offered her a drink, but she shook her head. Choosing the couch on the assumption that he would join her there, she had to hide her disappointment when he selected an armchair and started on his drink, contemplating her over the rim of the glass.

'About the wedding,' he said after a while, 'have you changed your mind about guests?'

Naomi shook her head. 'Except, perhaps, your father?'

He smiled reflectively at his glass. 'Not your own father, but mine. He'd be flattered. I've already invited him, together with his wife-to-be, but he hoped we would understand if they just sent their good wishes. They'll be marrying themselves in a few days. He wouldn't tell me the date, but I wished them well,' he looked across at her, 'from both of us.'

Naomi nodded, twisting her engagement ring. 'One thing I do know.' She studied the diamond. 'They'll be happier than we shall be.'

'That's a sweeping statement, don't you think?'

She met his eyes squarely. 'I don't think it is. Where your mother's concerned, your father's forgiven if not forgotten. But you hold a grudge against all women because of one woman—your mother.'

Gareth drained the glass and put it down, standing and pushing his fingers into his waistband. The action emphasised his leanness and aroused such powerful feelings of longing inside Naomi that she had to look down at her ring again.

'I'm not conscious of holding a grudge, but if I do, can you blame me?'

'After what I've done, you mean?' Her voice was touching on the shrill. 'After my irresponsibility in bringing into the world a baby who would never have had a proper family life if you hadn't offered to do your duty and marry me and adopt my child?'

'I couldn't have put it better myself.'

'You—you're ignorant and arrogant and insensitive and—and totally devoid of intelligence. I don't care if you have climbed up high on the academic ladder, your powers of deduction where human beings are concerned are nil. Nil, do you understand?'

He had turned pale under her avalanche of accusations. He grabbed her by the arms and swung her round. He could not have missed the desperation in her face. 'I feel like a hunted animal,' she cried, her heart pounding as if she were running for her own preservation, 'and you're the predator! You've torn me to pieces so much since the moment we saw each other again when I was with Brian and you knocked me down, that I don't want to marry you any more. You can speak the marriage vows with your girl-friend, Pam Hatton!'

He shook her until her teeth chattered and his fingers dug into her arms. 'Say you're sorry for that unpleasant little innuendo.'

'I'm s-sorry.' His hold slackened. 'Though I don't see why I should be, after all the nasty things you've said to me.' She paused, then added, 'But I still don't want to marry you.'

She was pulling at her ring when Garath stopped her. 'You'll marry me, and why? Because without me, you'd be lost. With me as your husband, you'll have a home, a father for your child, and no financial problems.' He broke contact with her, putting a distance between them. 'And I would never forgive myself for breaking the promise I made two years ago to marry you.'

He turned away. The discussion had ended. The gulf between them was wider than ever.

CHAPTER NINE

'How far have you got in tracing the whereabouts of your boy-friend?'

Gareth had come into the dining-room and was watching Naomi toying with her breakfast. Her appetite had lessened the nearer her wedding day came. He had told her he had eaten and had cleared away.

'If you mean Brian,' she repeated the words wearily, 'nowhere.'

Gareth frowned, tightening his belt a notch. 'Isn't there anyone else you can ask? I don't want to pay someone to track him down if it can be avoided. It goes against the grain to use secretive methods.'

'You're such an upstanding, honourable member of society, aren't you?' she commented aggressively. Her stormy eyes met his and she felt the cut of flint in them. 'Believing in me as you do.'

'I'll overlook the sarcasm,' he grated, 'but the answer to your question is yes, I am, since tomorrow I'm legally taking you on board. There are two reasons.' His cold eyes raked her, and he did not bother to keep the lust from them. 'First, you get under my skin. You're the woman I desire physically above all others.'

'Thank you, kind sir, for such subtly-phrased compliments!'

His answer was a scathing look before his gaze swept across the room to the baby cooing happily on a rug.

'Secondly,' he continued, 'since it's in my power to offer a mother and her baby shelter and comfort, and the child every educational advantage she cares to take in the future, I'm doing just that. Without any sense of self-sacrifice, I might add, because of the rewards I'll receive in other ways from the mother who will be my wife.'

Naomi turned on him. 'Need you be so cold-blooded about it all? And as for offering shelter and comfort, you sound as if you're offering state benefits under a social welfare programme! If only you'd——' She was unable to finish the sentence. Her voice wavered and broke and she covered her face with her hands. The silent tears trickled down her cheeks and she wished from the depths of her being that things could be different.

An arm across her shoulders was no compensation for all the misery its owner's intransigent attitude had inflicted on her. 'All right,' she mumbled, shaking the arm away, feeling it return at once, 'so you've got high moral standards. So have I, only you won't allow yourself to acknowledge the fact.'

Gareth's arm turned her, pulling her close. At first she resisted, but its offer of warmth and security, like his offer of marriage, was too wonderful to refuse. Her head lowered to rest against him. When she had calmed to quietness, he put a finger to her chin and dried her damp face.

'I'll try Brian's mother,' Naomi said at last. 'If he's given anyone his address, surely it would be her?'

He nodded and put her from him. She pocketed his handkerchief, saying she would wash it, then looked up at him, her smile as watery as her eyes.

'Sorry,' she whispered, and saw a curious flicker in his gaze. She looked away to give her heartbeats time to resume their normal beat. 'Have you remembered the ring?'

He nodded, pulling a box from his hip pocket. It was then that she realised how good he was looking. His deep brown shirt matched the colour of his well-cut trousers. The stretch-strap of his watch clasped his strong wrist below the buttoned shirt cuff. Was he going places? To the university, perhaps?

Gareth removed the gold band from the box. 'Try it on. If it doesn't fit, I've got time to change it today.'

Without removing her engagement ring, she slipped the band of gold on top of it. 'It fits,' she confirmed, handing it back.

'Good.' He pushed the box back into his pocket when the doorbell rang.

Naomi frowned, putting a hand to her flushed cheek. 'Are you expecting anyone?'

'It should be Pam Hatton. Did I forget to tell you? Before I answer the door, have you decided what to do about Becky while we're away from the house tomorrow?'

'My parents will have to have her. It won't be for long.'

The doorbell rang again. 'Have you asked them?'

'No question of asking. They'll just have to agree.'

His shoulders lifted noncommittally. 'You know them best.'

'Yes, I do.' Naomi frowned, turning away. 'It's about time they took some of the responsibility on their shoulders.' She had spoken mainly to herself, the words covered by a third and very impatient demand for entry.

'What did you say?' Gareth asked from the door.

'You'd better let your lady friend in,' she retorted, and smiled at his thrusting, angry jaw.

As soon as Gareth had gone, Naomi washed the dishes and rang Brian's mother.

'I'm so pleased to hear from you, dear,' Mrs Westley exclaimed. 'How's my lovely grandchild? Where are you staying, at your parents' place?'

'Becky's fine, Mrs Westley, and no, I'm not living

with my parents. My mother probably wouldn't have minded, but my father——'

'He's a bit difficult, dear? Yes, I know how some men can be funny about these things. So where are you and Becky living, dear?' There was curiosity in her voice, and puzzlement.

This would be difficult, Naomi thought. 'With an—I mean at the house of an—an old friend, Mrs Westley.' She hurried on, hoping Mrs Westley's curiosity would not demand to know the name of that friend, 'It's a very nice house, and there's everything we could possibly need here.'

'So your friend doesn't mind the baby being there? How lovely. Well, I'm glad to know you're both settled in so nicely, especially after being turned out of your other place.'

'Before you go, Mrs Westley,' Naomi interposed hurriedly, 'do you happen to know Brian's address?'

There was an uncertain pause and Naomi closed her eyes, thinking, Please, please say you do!

'Well, he has written, dear,' she answered at last, 'but he keeps saying he's moving around so much it's no use telling me exactly where he's staying, only the town. No, Naomi, sorry I can't help you, dear.' She added, 'Is there any special reason why you wanted to contact him?'

'Just—just to tell him——' Naomi moistened her lips, 'that I'm getting married tomorrow.'

'My word,' Mrs Westley responded happily, 'you've kept that a big secret! I'm so glad for you.' The words ceased. A thought had come to her. 'What about Becky?'

'Oh, she'll be all right for the day. I'll be taking her round to my parents' house.' Had her deliberate obtuseness put Brian's mother off the scent? To Naomi's disappointment, it seemed not.

'Oh, good. But that's not what I meant, Naomi. I

mean, once you've married, what will happen to Becky?'

'My—my fiancé doesn't mind at all about her, Mrs Westley. We shall be carrying on together, Becky and I. She'll live with us, you see.' In no circumstances, Naomi decided, could she tell the baby's grandmother that her husband-to-be insisted on adopting her son's child.

'Well, that's a relief. Isn't it wonderful of him not to mind someone else's baby in his house? It means Clare can carry on with her career, doesn't it?'

'And Brian won't have the worry of looking after a young baby,' Naomi added her own reassurances. Clare, she thought, always Clare and her precious career, not about my own sacrifices, not at all about the baby's needs.

'That's quite right. Well, if Brian does contact me, I'll tell him your news. I'm sure he'll be delighted.'

'And would you please ask him to contact me, Mrs Westley? Could you take my address, then he can write to me here.'

Naomi dictated Gareth's address, after which Mrs Westley again offered her good wishes and rang off.

Turning to the recumbent but lively baby, Naomi held out her arms, dropped to her knees and scooped up the warm, human bundle. She smiled at the little girl, picking out her sister's characteristics one by one. Becky saw the smile and reciprocated. There was something the baby could not interpret—a hard, shining look which told of her aunt's inner bitterness.

From upstairs there came laughter, the scraping back of a chair, a book falling to the floor. Naomi stiffened and felt jealousy eating at her very roots, slowly killing her.

'You,' she told Becky, 'and I are going places, doing things, seeing people. Come on, little one, we're taking action! And,' she whispered in the baby's ear just before she climbed the stairs, 'you can be quite sure of one thing. Your Aunt Naomi will never desert you as your true parents have done.'

Outside Gareth's room, Naomi paused, hesitated, looked down into Becky's face, then opened the door. Two heads shot round, one lifting from reading a book on a table, the other from staring at that book over a broad, hard shoulder.

Gareth's eyes went narrowly from Naomi to Becky. 'What the hell do you want?' he snapped.

Naomi saw a young, slim girl wearing jeans and round-necked white shirt. Her hair was blonde, streaked with a darker shade. It was lifted high into a knot, yet carelessly fixed, since strands hung down. Her face was pixie-pointed, her eyes brightly alert, her smile wide and welcoming. Just as I imagined her to be, Naomi thought.

Most of all, Naomi saw how near she was standing to the man who was, in twenty-four hours' time, to become her own husband.

Right, she decided, they've all laid at my feet Clare's errors and Clare's responsibilities. So I'll *be* Clare. I'll become star of the show.

'Miss Hatton?' she asked over-sweetly. 'How nice to meet you, not that Gareth's introduced us.' She moved into the room, indicating with her head the baby in her arms. 'Don't you think Gareth and I have been clever? Isn't she beautiful, our baby?'

She paused to glance at a bemused young woman and in doing so, was unable to miss Gareth's incensed response.

'I can see Gareth hasn't breathed a word to you,' Naomi continued, pleased at discovering that she, too, had acting ability. 'It's been a complete secret until now, but we're getting married tomorrow, so it doesn't matter who knows, even you.'

'Naomi!' Gareth had risen.

Ignoring the warning in his tone, Naomi persisted, 'Becky won't be at the wedding, of course. It just isn't done, even in these liberated days, to bring the baby an unwed couple has produced to the wedding ceremony.'

'If you——'

'Darling,' Naomi cut across Gareth's second warning, 'I'm off to see my parents. I'm certain they'll agree to have our darling offspring while we're being married.'

'I—I didn't know you were getting married, Gareth,' Pam Hatton sought for a disclaimer from the man on whose shoulder her hand was now resting, 'er—Miss——' She removed her hand quickly.

'Call me Naomi, Miss Hatton. Everybody does.' Her over-wide smile began to hurt her jaws. 'Tomorrow at——' She was almost stumped. He had not told her. 'Ask Gareth. But there'll be no guests. It's going to be very, very quiet.'

She looked again at Becky. 'Isn't it, darling? And all because of you. But this time tomorrow, my pet, you'll have a real daddy, won't you? He's real now, of course, standing over there, looking so angry, but tomorrow, he'll be legally responsible for both of us. Oh well,' Naomi flashed a brilliant look at her husband-to-be, 'we must go. So glad to have met you, Miss Hatton. 'Bye, darling . . . Gareth . . .'

Her words faded out, but the moment before she withdrew, her eyes seeking his grew haunted and her false smile trembled to nothing.

'Mother, there's no one else I can ask to have Becky. I don't know the neighbours, Gareth's father's gone away again.'

Sybil Pemberton was holding her head. 'You've told me so many things in such a short time. Give me a few moments to sort them all out.'

Becky was alseep in the garden, her grandfather was out at his place of work. Naomi and her mother had almost finished morning coffee.

'Now,' said Sybil, settling back in the chair, 'can you go through it all again? You and Gareth are getting married tomorrow.'

Naomi nodded. 'No guests, Mum, no reception.'

'But why, dear, why? You've done nothing wrong. In fact, you've been very good, really.' Sybil spoke as if the fact had just occurred to her—which was probably the truth, Naomi thought acidly.

'You try convincing Gareth that I've done nothing wrong! I've told him till my voice has almost gone hoarse, but still he won't believe me.'

'Right, I will,' Sybil pronounced with unusual firmness. 'He'll be told the truth and nothing else from me. What's his number?'

Naomi wrote it down, giving it to her mother, watching fascinatedly as her mother went into the hall and dialled. Sybil's face smiled as she appeared to receive an answer, then it frowned, covering the mouthpiece.

'It's a woman,' she whispered, 'did you know he had a woman with him?'

Naomi nodded, suppressing a smile.

'What?' Sybil was saying. 'Do I want Gareth? Yes, I do want Gareth. Who are you?' Luckily, it seemed that the one who had answered had gone.

Still slightly stupefied, Naomi listened. After all her unhappiness, all the embittered talk, was this to be her moment of release?

'Gareth?' Sybil's voice was still slightly scolding. 'It's about Naomi. No, there's nothing wrong with her. I mean, all the things you've been accusing her of, like being the baby's mother, are all lies. Yes, lies. She's no more the baby's mother than I am. It's Clare who gave birth to Becky, not Naomi. Now do you understand?'

There was a pause. Sybil listened intently, then said, 'You do understand? That's wonderful! Thank goodness we've cleared that up. Yes, Naomi's here.' Sybil held out the receiver, her face beaming. 'He wants to talk to you. Don't worry, I've cleared the whole matter up.'

Naomi whispered, 'Yes?'

'Conspiracy will get you nowhere,' she heard, and the phone was rammed down in her ear.

Naomi stood for a moment with her back to her mother. She was trying to control the trembling movement of her lips. At last she turned, having tightened her mouth into a smile. 'Thank you, Mother. He understood.'

'Oh, good. Now, let's carry on discussing the arrangements. You'll bring Becky here first thing.' She frowned sharply. 'I wish you'd let your father and me come to the wedding. It will be our first marriage in the family.'

'Clare gave you your first grandchild, but you didn't go wild about that.'

'There's no need to be nasty about your sister, dear.'

'It wasn't my sister I was talking about.' Naomi stopped, shaking her head. It was hopeless. How could she communicate with a mother and father who had tunnel vision where their two daughters were concerned? They could see only Clare, Clare and her theatrical achievements, Clare, in whose reflected glory they were living.

'I'll bring everything you need for feeding Becky. Can you remember how to bottle-feed a baby, Mother?'

Sybil fluttered her hands. 'How can I remember, dear, when I fed both you and Clare myself?'

Naomi sighed, 'I'll bring you the instruction book,' she answered, smiling in spite of herself, thinking that it sounded like a piece of equipment they were talking about, not a small human being who could be as awkward as the rest of them when she liked.

'Nappies—you'll bring those, won't you?' Sybil asked the question anxiously. 'Now I do remember all about those—I think.'

'If you've forgotten,' Naomi soothed, smiling widely, 'Dad can remind you how.'

Sybil was nodding when she realised what her daughter had said. 'Your father? He doesn't know one end of a baby from the other!' Mother and daughter shared a moment's joyous laughter.

At the turn of the key in the lock, the laughter ended. 'Your father, dear, home for the afternoon.'

On cue, Becky began to cry. Naomi thought, Gareth was right about Becky having her mother's instinct for timing. John Pemberton appeared at the living-room door, glaring at his daughter.

'Why have you brought your niece to the house again? Are you trying to get round us to let you and that baby live here?'

'Thanks for those few kind words, Dad,' Naomi returned, as mildly as her annoyance would allow, 'but I'm not trying to persuade you and Mum to lumber yourselves with our presence. All the same, you'll have to get used to having her here all day tomorrow, because Gareth and I are getting married.'

Her father, it seemed, needed both a drink and a seat. Unable to do both at once, he poured the drink first, his hand appearing to shake a little, then sank carefully into the nearest armchair, which happened to be opposite his wife's.

'Isn't this short notice?' he demanded, having taken a gulp of liquid. 'I'm taking this afternoon off, so I can't have tomorrow as well. Now, if you'd left it to the weekend . . . However, your mother can go. She loves weddings, and I'll be here for the reception.'

'I'm sorry, Father, but you're not invited to the wedding. Nor is Mum. And as I said before, there'll be no reception. Gareth and I will come straight back here after the ceremony and collect Becky. We may have a meal somewhere, I suppose. It——' she gave her father a sideways look, noting his uncomprehending expression, 'it depends on how generous Gareth is feeling. Towards me, I mean, not financially.'

'Oh, but I've told him now, dear. He knows Becky's not your baby. He said he understood.'

Her mother's naïvety made Naomi smile. 'Thank you, Mother, but Gareth understands exactly what he wants to understand.'

Sybil shook her head. 'I don't follow you, dear.'

John's head had been swivelling from one to the other, and it seemed to Naomi that he did not follow her, either. Becky's crying, which had subsided, began again, this time in earnest. John swallowed his drink and covered his ears.

'I'll get her in,' Naomi announced, and promptly did so, wheeling in the carrycot and leaving it in the hall.

Becky was using her arms and legs to express her irritation at being so neglected. 'She's got all her mother's characteristics, not just some,' her aunt commented, holding out the baby to her grandmother.

Sybil took her gladly. Becky calmed down, having a new set of human features to study. Her grandmother's happy smile produced a beatific one on her own face. Grandmother laughed, grandchild chuckled. It makes a beautiful picture, Naomi thought, going to the fridge for the baby's bottle and warming it gently.

There had been no sarcasm in her mind as the thought had come, but the bitterness it aroused because of the circumstances in which she was the still, unchanging centre nearly broke her heart.

As the white liquid in the bottle disappeared inside his daughter's love child, John Pemberton stared, fascinated. His so-called high standards, Naomi pondered as she watched the contentment on her niece's face, had long ago crumbled in the face of simple, unadulterated human warmth.

Judging by his expression, he was fast growing to love his grandchild, and Naomi was glad, not for her sister's sake, but the baby's. One day, one day, she thought, when Gareth and I . . . But, she checked the wonderful idea, he'll never love me enough to want me to have his children.

Her mind changed gear and her thoughts slowed down. One day, maybe I'll go away somewhere, just to be on my own, away from Gareth's suspicions, away from people who are constantly taking advantage of me. If I ever did, Becky can be sure of having two people who will love her and care for her until she's old enough to understand. To understand exactly what, Naomi did not let herself reflect.

Gareth met her at the front door. He was there opening it before she could find her key. She pushed the carrycot over the threshold.

'Where the hell have you been?' he demanded.

It was, Naomi decided sourly, getting just a little monotonous. Her glance flicked up the stairs. She could, if she liked, say the same to him.

'You know where—at my parents'. I stayed for the evening meal. I'd taken Becky's things, enough for the day. Anyway,' she lifted a tired Becky from the carrycot, 'I'm sure you weren't lonely.'

He folded his arms, his eyes openly mocking. 'No, I wasn't. I enjoyed every minute of Pam's visit. We worked, of course, and we—talked.'

The hesitation was sufficient, Naomi thought

furiously, to tell a book-length tale. She swung to the stairs. 'I'm putting Becky to bed.'

Gareth did not answer. She walked up, each step heavier than the other. Hating the idea that he might read the unhappy state of her mind by the slowness of her tread, she quickened her pace, but it was a painful exercise.

Gareth was wandering around the sitting-room when she went down after putting Becky to bed. She watched him from the door, but he did not look at her. Was he thinking about Pam Hatton and of his relationship with her after tomorrow?

'Do you want to back out?' Naomi asked, finding a seat.

'From what?'

'Marrying me tomorrow.'

He stood still in front of her. 'What makes you ask?'

He had spoken so coldly, she wished she had not raised the matter. 'Maybe it was your answer on the telephone this morning.'

He shook his head as if she were a slow-thinking child. 'Didn't it occur to you how obvious it was? You went to your mother asking for her help in persuading me to change my mind about your relationship to the baby. She gave you that help. I don't blame her and I don't blame you.'

'That makes a change,' she flashed at him.

'For trying, I mean,' he returned over-patiently. 'But it made no difference. I'm not that much of a fool.'

'I'm glad you admit that, percentage-wise, you're a bit of one.'

He came menacingly towards her. 'You think you're clever, don't you?'

She sighed. 'Not very. In fact, I admit I'm a fool from top to toe.' Her gaze challenged his. 'But you—you're as smug and self-opinionated and bound by your traditional ways of thinking as my father is about convention and so-called moral codes. At least *he* seems to be changing at long last.'

'Meaning?' The icy anger in his eyes frightened her.

'That you accept circumstantial evidence as the truth without even questioning it and that you refuse to make use of your human instincts and intuition instead of your cold powers of reasoning. *That's* what I mean.'

'So in your opinion where your behaviour is concerned, I should forgive and forget, as you say my father has done towards my mother?'

'Gareth,' she cried, 'there's nothing to forgive *or* forget!'

He pivoted and made straight for the door. She ran after him as he strode up the stairs. 'Gareth.' He slowed down. 'We'll have to have witnesses, won't we. What shall we do—ask a couple of strangers?'

'A colleague of mine has agreed to act in that capacity.'

'But we shall need two. Will he bring his wife?'

'No. She will bring her husband. And,' he continued walking, 'her name is Jill Wainwright, not Pam Hatton.'

Naomi spent a lonely wedding eve trying to watch television. She could hear Gareth moving around upstairs and tried her best to will him down to share the creeping hours with her. He did not come.

Going up to bed, she took her wedding outfit from the wardrobe, inspecting it for creases. There were none, and she put it back. After two hours, she gave up all pretence of trying to sleep. Worries about the step she was taking pressed down on her mind.

Would the time ever come when Gareth believed in her, and if that time did, would his love for her, if by now he felt any at all, have died beyond resuscitation?

Sitting up and switching on the table lamp, she

reached for a book and opened it. After reading for a while, her attention wandered and she wondered how Gareth could manage to sleep as he must have been doing by now, since there had been no sound from him. Was he not troubled in any way by the responsibilities he was taking on?

Snapping the book shut, she got up and pattered to the window, pulling aside the curtain. When would Brian contact her, and when he did, would he give his consent to the adoption? And if he didn't, what then?

In the reflection from the darkened window pane, she watched mesmerised as the door was opened. Gareth was wearing pyjama trousers with a shirt hanging open across his shoulders. His hair was ruffled as though tired fingers had pushed through it. Had he been working in order to pass the time? Had he been unable to sleep, too?

Naomi turned, saw his shadowed eyes and knew the answer.

He lifted up his arms. 'Would these be any use to you?' His shirt had opened wide, showing the lean line of him.

'If me in them would be any use to you,' she whispered, a shy half-smile meeting the intensity of his gaze.

'You're saying that to please me?'

She nodded, then added, 'It would please me, too.'

He shrugged away his shirt and looked again at his arms. 'Then why aren't you in them?'

Running across the room, she threw herself against him and was at once enclosed in his hold. His cheek came down, resting on her hair. His fingers pushed upwards inside its dark strands and pressed her head against his chest.

Her nails ran gently through his chest hairs, her lips turned to kiss them, wriggling her nose as they tickled, making her laugh up at him. His eyes told her an unreadable message, gleaming in the semi-darkness.

Naomi stilled against him, her breath coming deeply. 'It's a mess, such an awful mess,' she mumbled, her lips to his skin. 'If only . . .' A deep sigh racked her. 'I spend my life saying that.'

'If only you loved me?' His voice floated over her head.

'That isn't in doubt.' She pulled away to look at him.

'No, that I can't believe. And don't ask me why.'

'Because you'll tell me, and it will be the same old story—me plus Brian equals Becky. Right?'

'Right.'

'Wrong. Oh, what's the use? Here we go again!' She tugged to get away but he tugged her back.

'What was all that about this morning when Pam was here? She knows Becky isn't ours, couldn't possibly be. I was working with her for nearly two years, remember.'

'So?' She did not look at him but stayed with her cheek close to his warm, muscled flesh. 'You could have slipped away one weekend without telling her, couldn't you?'

He was quiet for a long time. 'You're still jealous of her?' he remarked at last.

Now she jerked away. 'Why shouldn't I be? There she was, being all lovey-dovey with you, nestling up to you as though it was her you were going to marry tomorrow, not me. Anyway,' before he could reply, 'I was fed up with being pushed around by everybody, and that includes you!'

His laugh was low and she felt its vibrations. His feet moved, bringing her closer. His fingers forced her buttons open, the nightgown was at her feet and he was carrying her to the bed.

He looked her over like a swordsman admiring the

length and sharpness of his shining blade. 'As of now,' he lay beside her, 'I'm going to push you around for the rest of my life.'

He rolled her round towards him and his hands moulded her breasts. 'You're so beautiful,' he said, 'with a face so lovely, eyes so trusting, I can scarcely believe——' Her hand stopped the words before they reached his lips. Then a yawn overtook her, making her shake. He kissed her fingers and moved them from his mouth. 'Turn around. You're so tired it would be cruelty to wives to indulge my desire for you tonight.'

'What about my desire?' she asked mischievously over her shoulder.

'Cheeky little kitten! After tomorrow, we'll have all our lives for that.' He kissed her shoulder. 'Sleep now, Naomi,' he commanded softly. 'I want a radiant bride tomorrow.'

Naomi smiled. As she was closing her eyes, already halfway to sleeping, she heard him whisper from the start of his dream,

'I still love you, in spite of . . . your . . . treachery.'

Tears came because his words had confirmed that even now he had not forgiven her for what he believed she had done. Her cheeks were still damp when she awoke momentarily in the night, turning into his waiting arms.

Waking at six-thirty to a sunlit morning, Naomi grew conscious of being the only occupant of the bed. Scrambling out, she made for the shower cubicle adjoining her bedroom, emerging refreshed.

The mirror showed her a rounded, happy face holding all the radiance her fiancé could have wished for. Pulling on cords and blouse, she ran downstairs to greet him. He was not there. A note stood on the kitchen table, supported by a jug.

'Naomi,' it said, 'I'll pick you up at your parents' house at eleven-thirty.'

With little appetite, Naomi ate the two pieces of toast she had made for herself, drank the coffee with as little enthusiasm and washed the dishes.

Her movements had disturbed Becky and she went to her, lifting and cuddling her. She held her high and the baby chuckled. Bringing her down, Naomi whispered, 'I'm marrying Gareth this morning, darling. Soon you'll be getting a daddy, a proper daddy. Soon . . .'

As she dressed her, Naomi talked. 'Your granny can feed you today. I'll have to teach her how. Isn't that strange, when she's had two children of her own? It isn't really, you know, because your mother should have fed you herself, instead of using a bottle, then walking off and leaving you.'

Putting into Brian's car enough, she told herself, to see Becky through for a week, Naomi lowered her on to the back seat. Then, with great care, she draped her wedding outfit over the back of the passenger seat.

True to tradition, she would change at her parents' house and leave from there for her wedding, even though it was her husband-to-be who would be taking her. Even now, she did not regret the lack of fuss. In the unusual circumstances, anything elaborate would have seemed entirely wrong.

John Pemberton met his daughter on the doorstep. His eyes were just a little wary as he looked at his grandchild but her unwavering gaze as it rested on him was not followed by an open baby-mouth emitting an ear-splitting scream. He relaxed visibly and even smiled.

Naomi did not hide her amusement at the sight of the tall, white-haired man revealing the inner apprehension which the mere appearance of his tiny grandchild evinced.

Her mother was seated on the couch, clean apron in place, hands scrubbed, waiting for the baby to be lowered into her arms. Sybil did not need much tuition. After a few minutes it all seemed to come to her naturally.

Noticing her father hovering, Naomi remarked, 'I thought you'd be at work today, Dad?'

'He changed his mind, dear,' her mother answered for him, patting a surprisingly biddable Becky on the back.

'Your mother insisted,' John put in on his own behalf. 'Since she's decided to come to your wedding whether you want her there or not, it was left to me to act as baby-minder.' His wary look, as he regarded his elder daughter's child, was back. 'I hope this updated version of Clare doesn't give as much trouble as her mother did at that age.'

'I wasn't around at that particular time,' Naomi replied dryly, 'but if you treat Becky right, she's as good as gold.' She grinned up at her father.

John gave a grunt and walked away.

'It will be only for an hour or so, won't it, dear?' his wife soothed.

Naomi nodded. 'Becky's usually very good once she's asleep. Makes no sound, until she wakes,' Naomi added with another smile. 'You'll have to be as quiet as a mouse yourself, won't you, and not wake her until Mother comes back.'

'Now, you run upstairs to your old room, dear,' Sybil instructed her daughter, 'and change into your new dress. I can manage this lovely baby quite well.'

Naomi, who had been able, until that moment, to hold her mounting excitement at bay, felt her heartbeats gaining pace. Half an hour later, she was down again.

Her mother had changed, too, and both women praised each other's taste.

'You look quite radiant, Naomi,' her mother commented warmly, hugging her daughter. 'And so beautiful I think Gareth might eat you!'

Naomi laughed, her tension slackening a little. She thought, but did not say, Gareth could make a meal out of me any day he chooses, and I love him so much, I wouldn't have the power to stop him.

Finding her mouth was dry and wondering why she was so apprehensive since she had spent the night in her fiancé's arms, she went into the kitchen for a glass of water. She heard her mother say,

'Now you take care of that lovely grandchild of ours, John.'

John answered in subservient, suitably lamb-like tones, 'I'll guard her better than a well-trained Alsatian dog!'

Having slaked her thirst, Naomi smiled. Among all the other things she had done for Clare, she had reconciled their father to the baby to whom he had not so long ago denied a home and would, had he been able to, have denied her very existence.

It seemed that hours had passed since she had seen Gareth. His car came to a stop in the drive next to Brian's. As he got out, he looked disparagingly at the older car's battered state.

Sybil was at the door to greet him. As Naomi stood in the shadows, she was rewarded by the sight of Gareth's eyes searching for her. Having found her, he did not smile. Instead, he sent her a message—*you'll soon belong to me.*

It was her mother who occupied the front passenger seat. Naomi was content to sit in the back, staring out at the green fields and wondering how she would feel when they passed them on the journey back.

Gareth's two friends were delighted to meet her, they said, greeting her mother warmly, too. Out of nowhere came the thought that she was glad, after all, to have one of her parents at her wedding, especially her mother.

The ceremony was simple and, to Naomi, strangely moving. Marriage meant something, after all, in spite of its abuse by so many couples. Well, it meant something to her, anyway, she reasoned, feeling as enveloped by the feeling of love as her finger now did by Gareth's gold band.

It was impossible to tell from whom that 'love' emanated. Probably her mother, she reflected, but that thought did not stop her looking up with something near to adoration into Gareth's face. By the lift of his eyebrow, he was mocking her for it. 'Carried away by the special atmosphere,' she could almost hear him thinking. At that moment she did not care just how much her love for him showed.

Gareth grasped her hand as they emerged into the sunlight. He pulled her across the courtyard to stand in front of some flowering bushes.

A camera clicked and Naomi's head swung to see Gareth's colleague's husband taking photographs. 'Photography's my hobby,' he called to Naomi. 'You don't object to my using you as models, I hope?'

'I'll whisper it,' his wife called, 'but Gareth especially asked him to do this. Now the bride's mother,' she added, motioning to Sybil to join her daughter and new son-in-law.

'And another,' her husband coaxed. 'Now the bride and bridegroom may kiss.'

While everyone laughed, Gareth obliged with speed, putting his hands on her shoulders and pulling her to him. There was another click of the camera.

Gareth had arranged for them to have a meal, having booked lunch at an expensive hotel on the outskirts of the town. The Tudor beams hung low, brasses gleamed. Other people came and went, but Naomi was conscious only of the presence of her new husband, and of the sweet perfume rising from the shoulder spray which he had given her just before the wedding.

It was past two o'clock when they arrived back at Naomi's parents' house. Her first thought was for Becky. Hurrying ahead, she pushed at the door, expecting it to resist. It came open.

In the hall, her father was waiting. His face was white and he was shaking. Naomi's first thought was that he was ill, but he shook his head.

'It's Becky,' he said hoarsely. 'She's gone from her cot. Someone's taken her!'

CHAPTER TEN

GARETH and Sybil had joined them. Sybil went across to stand beside her husband. There was an unbelieving silence.

'How could you, Father, how could you?' Naomi accused. Her own body was shaking now. All her bridal radiance had drained away. 'I trusted you! You were left in charge of your own granddaughter, yet you——' Her eyes were dazed as she stared at him. 'You arranged it! You pretended to love her, yet you found that deep down, you still couldn't accept her!'

Conscious that her voice had risen towards hysteria, she caught it back on a choking sob. Her father was shaking his head. There was sadness in the movement and hopelessness, too.

'I thought *you* had arranged it, my dear.'

'Me?' she cried. 'To get her out of my life, you mean? How could you think that, oh, how could you?'

Gareth's hands on her shoulders shook her back from the brink of lost control. A sob shuddered through her and she found herself against him, crying all her wedding day happiness away. Then she tore free. She had started clutching at straws.

'Maybe you imagined it, Father. Maybe she's there now, in the carrycot, waiting.' Before she could be stopped, she was away through to the kitchen and looking outside. The carrycot was not in its usual place. She searched around, finding it at last down the sideway, near the garden door.

It was as empty as her father had said. Becky had gone. The others had joined her. Frantically she searched the cot for clues. Everything had been taken, the covers, even the padded mattress on which she had lain.

All the time, Naomi was sobbing. When Gareth attempted to calm her, she shook herself free.

'What is it doing here, John?' she heard her mother ask, 'instead of in front of the sitting-room doors?'

'I was working at the end of the garden,' he explained. 'I wheeled her here in case I dropped the spade or something and woke her. Naomi said,' he looked resentfully at his daughter, 'that she wouldn't wake up unless she was disturbed.'

'So you used the peace and quiet to get on with your work?' Sybil asked. When her husband nodded, she added, 'Well, you can't be blamed for that.'

'Blamed or not,' Naomi took her up, 'it comes to the same thing. Becky's been stolen!'

'Wouldn't kidnapped be a more appropriate word?' Gareth's edged question made her turn.

'Are you accusing me of complicity again?' she cried, taking immediate offence. 'Do you honestly believe I'd be capable of arranging such a thing? First Father, now you! It's your turn, Mother. What else have I done to earn this low opinion of my character by those who ought to know me and love me best?'

A tense silence greeted her remark.

Sybil broke it. 'It's your wedding day, darling,' Sybil moaned, returning to the house. 'And we were all so happy!'

Indoors, they all found seats except Gareth, who seemed to prefer to stand. John said, 'We'll have to contact the police.'

Gareth's hand lifted and his hard stare was on his wife. 'Would you by any chance connect this act with Becky's father?'

Naomi gripped the chair arms. 'You mean Brian? Why should he——?' He loves her, she had said before, so wouldn't that apply now?

Gareth followed up his apparent advantage. 'Don't I recall his saying, "Nobody's going to adopt my child?" '

Into the silence came the ring of the telephone. Naomi was out of the chair and saying, 'I'll take it.'

She listened hard, hearing no words but a series of gurgles. 'B-Becky?' she stammered wonderingly into the mouthpiece. 'Is Becky there somebody? Who's calling? For heaven's sake, tell me. Is it—is it Brian?'

'It's Brian,' came the voice, 'and it's Becky. And it's me, Naomi, saying I'm sorry, really sorry I had to do this and spoil your wedding day. But there was no way I could stand around and watch my Becky being adopted. She's mine, Naomi. I know you love her, but she's mine.'

'Okay, Brian—I understand. I only hope you know how to look after her.'

'Don't worry about that. I've got books to tell me, and I remember watching you. She's grown a bit since I saw her, hasn't she? I think she's got a bit of me in her now, wouldn't you say?'

'Yes, Brian,' Naomi laughed and the relief came flooding, 'she's got a look of you in her, no doubt about it. 'Bye, Brian. Okay, you're sorry. So am I. You—you don't know what you've done to me.'

As she rang off, she turned—to find Gareth standing behind her.

'So my guess—and your father's—was right.' The words dropped like icicles down her back. 'An arranged job.'

Looking up at him, she saw such a look of condemnation on his face she could not stand it. Taking up her bag from the floor where she had dropped it on entry, she ran outside, let herself into Brian's car and drove away.

Reason had told her that Gareth would take his leave of her parents before following her. This time her reason let her down. He was on her tail all the way back, through winding country lanes and small areas of open roads.

Naomi did not even see the fields she had contemplated on the way in. Had she done so, she would have realised that before the ceremony it would not have occurred to her that she might look upon those fields now with fear in her heart.

Braking to a crash stop in Gareth's driveway, she scampered to the front door, scrabbling in her bag for the keys. He was there behind her, reaching over to unlock the door.

He pushed her in, closed it and turned the searchlight of his eyes upon her innermost being. Remote, icy-cold, was he seeking out the truth at last? To her deeply unhappy mind he did not seem like a man on the edge of a miraculous discovery.

Gripping his arm, she shook it. 'For heaven's sake,' she exclaimed, 'you married me today! You must have had some trust in me to have given me your name and your roof over my head!'

Still Gareth gazed back at her, silent and unmoved.

'Oh, yes, I remember now,' she went on with heavy sarcasm, 'a form of social welfare, wasn't it? Your duty as a good citizen to come to the aid of an unmarried mother, not to mention your biological need for my——'

He gripped her shoulders. 'Be quiet, or I'll do something drastic to make you come to your senses!'

'Such as throwing me out on the street now there's no child to consider? It was all a waste of time marrying me, wasn't it? Now the baby's gone . . .'

It hit her then, the silence, the emptiness, the lack of someone to care for, someone to love.

With shaking fingers she unpinned the spray of flowers. Going towards the stairs, she noticed that Gareth was picking up a letter. It must have been lying there unnoticed while they quarrelled. Since he opened it, she assumed the letter was for him.

There was an empty vase on the windowsill of her bedroom. Putting the spray into it, she filled the vase with water and replaced it on the sill. Dispiritedly she looked at her reflection, then looked quickly away. She could not bear to see the dullness in her own eyes.

Stretching behind her to unfasten the zip, she reached halfway, only to discover that its movement had been taken over from her. She stiffened, feeling the dress being slipped from her shoulders and freed from her arms.

Two strong hands swung her round and she opened her mouth to protest. Two blazing eyes burned into hers—but there was no anger in them, nor condemnation. They held instead all the things she had longed to see from the moment they had been reunited.

Admiration was there, respect and esteem. Was there also—or had she imagined it—the merest trace of regard? From his pocket he took a piece of paper. Naomi recognised it at once. It was Becky's birth certificate. Clare had not let her down, after all!

Naomi clasped her hands in sheer delight. 'You know now, you know the truth?'

His hands slipped to her waist and Naomi stepped out of her dress.

'I know now,' he answered.

'And you accept it as the truth?'

'I accept it as the truth.'

'Gareth—oh, Gareth!' Her arms reached up to clasp around his neck.

They stood for a long time, holding each other, then he said against her neck, 'There's a letter from your sister addressed to both of us.' That, too, came from his pocket and Naomi took it eagerly. 'I read it, but it's really for you,' he added.

'Forgive me, Naomi,' it began, then Naomi found

herself pulled unceremoniously on to Gareth's lap as he occupied the cushioned bedroom chair. His arms settled more closely around her and his lips moved slowly over her bare shoulder. 'Now you can read it,' he allowed, with a gleam in his eye. 'While you're occupied, I'll be preoccupied.' There was no way of doubting his meaning.

Curling up in Gareth's lap, she lifted the letter, only to catch her breath as exploring, insistent fingers probed the lacy top of her silky underslip. They came to rest in the deep cleft between her breasts and she breathed again.

'Forgive me for being so bitchy towards you,' the letter continued. 'Becky's safe and with us both. Sorry Brian had to do it cloak-and-dagger style, but I didn't want it generally known—that I had a baby—until Brian and I were married. We're marrying secretly tomorrow.'

'Oh, dear,' Naomi commented, smiling and resting her head back on Gareth's shoulder, 'that won't be popular in the family! My parents' "famous" daughter——'

Gareth's mouth closed hers so effectively, her arms lifted to cross beneath his now-opened shirt. His hand was straying, stroking her ankle, her calves. While she had the strength, she pulled free, saying,

'Let me finish this letter, please, Gareth.'

Her large eyes pleaded and he laughed into them. He was the Gareth of old. The whole line of his face had softened, but most of all there was . . . something else. Was it the missing ingredient, the vital element for which she had been searching since his return into her life?

'Finish it,' he agreed, 'but if you're not quick about it, you'll be reading the end of it in a few hours' time. Or maybe,' her shoulder straps were slowly slipping, 'days from now.'

Naomi laughed, kissing his chin and resisting when he tried to grapple with her. His mouth found a resting place at the division of her breasts. 'You don't know what you're doing to me,' he muttered, 'keeping me waiting like this.'

Her own attention was acting waywardly, but she forced it back to the handwritten pages. 'We're sorry they won't have a "real" wedding in the family, as Mum would call it,' Clare continued, 'but at least they'll have a legitimate grandchild at last!

'Brian has been working with the theatrical company I belong to, making scenery and props. You know how good he is at his work. A final secret—I stayed with Brian whenever you went away for the weekend. I think I knocked over a bottle of your perfume, but didn't have time to pick it up.'

Yet there was I, Naomi thought, deciding that Mrs Westley had a liking for it and had used a few drops!

'So now you see,' Naomi read, 'why I was no stranger to Becky. I love her so much, Naomi, whatever all of you might think. Now things have settled down here and I'm on my way, I've got her with me. More seriously, there's no way I can find of making up to you for the trouble I caused between you and Gareth.'

Here, Naomi found that her husband was reading the letter with her. When his hand moved she squirmed at where it was resting.

'Nor of expressing my gratitude,' Naomi dragged her eyes back to the letter, 'to you for getting some sense into Dad and letting him and Becky get to know each other. All I can say is, thanks and thanks again. Clare.'

Naomi put the letter aside and settled down more securely on Gareth's lap. 'How do you think Clare would like it if I passed it to the press under the title of "Confessions of an Elder Sister"?'

'I think she'd tear you to little bits.'

Naomi shook her head, pulling at Gareth's chest hairs. 'I'm sure she'd love the publicity.' She tugged particularly hard and his hand slapped down on her thigh.

At her squeal of protest, he laughed and moved his palm upwards to rest intimately on her stomach. Her muscles contracted in sheer delight at his touch and she wrapped her arms around him. 'I love you, Gareth,' she whispered, her body on fire from his caresses. 'I wish you loved me back and not Pam Hatton.'

He pulled away in astonishment. 'You can't mean it? Pam's engaged to be married. He's a research assistant in my department, just a bit more senior to her. Didn't you know? Didn't you see her engagement ring?'

Naomi shook her head. 'You used her to make me jealous,' she accused.

'You saw only what your prejudiced eyes wanted to see. Isn't that right?'

'Maybe,' she temporised, hating to admit he was correct in his assessment of her state of mind.

'There's been no one else for me, do you know that?' he declared, pulling her closer. 'I've never stopped loving you from the moment we met. All through those two years, I cursed myself for being such a fool as to risk losing you. Yet my better judgment told me I'd acted wisely.'

Wide-eyed, Naomi gazed at him. 'You mean you loved me enough even to forgive me for what you were convinced I'd done?'

He nodded. 'There were times when I had deep doubts as to whether what you were telling me might be the truth.'

'Then something, or someone, did or said something which convinced you, after all, that I was in the wrong?'

'Unfortunately, yes. You must admit the cards were stacked against you.'

'It was terrible, Gareth. No matter how hard I tried, I just couldn't get through to you. Yet, all the time, you loved me?'

He nodded again. 'Enough even to adopt the child I thought you'd had. Okay, so I pretended it was to give you both shelter, but a man has his pride, and I'm no exception.'

Her eyes shone mischievously into his. 'Even pretending you loved me for my physical desirability?'

'But I do,' his head lowered and he kissed her rounded softness, 'the whole irresistible length of you. I want you, darling.' He stood up, lifting her with him. 'You've kept me waiting long enough.'

'Where are you taking me?' she asked dreamily, as he made for the door with her in his arms.

'My bedroom, which is where you belong.' He shouldered the door open and stood looking down at her. 'You're part of me, my love. I'm incomplete without you.' He lowered her on to the bed, joining her there.

'Come, love me,' she whispered on a quick breath.

'Just try and stop me,' he said roughly against her lips. 'And afterwards, I'll love you again.'

She knew then that all through their lives together, the loving would never stop. Which, she thought hazily, surrendering to his demanding lips, was what life was all about.

A very special gift for Mother's Day

You love Mills & Boon romances. Your mother will love this attractive Mother's Day gift pack. First time in paperback, four superb romances by leading authors. A very special gift for Mother's Day.

United Kingdom £4.40 — On sale from 24th Feb 1984

A Grand Illusion
Maura McGiveny

Desire in the Desert
Mary Lyons

Sensual Encounter
Carole Mortimer

Aquamarine
Madeleine Ker

Look for this gift pack where you buy Mills & Boon romances.

ROMANCE

Next month's romances from Mills & Boon

Each month, you can choose from a world of variety in romance with Mills & Boon. These are the new titles to look out for next month.

FIGHTING LADY Elizabeth Oldfield
INFATUATION Charlotte Lamb
THE WINGED LION Madeleine Ker
YESTERDAY'S SHADOW Helen Bianchin
IMPERFECT CHAPERONE Catherine George
KISS YESTERDAY GOODBYE Leigh Michaels
NEW DISCOVERY Jessica Ayre
PASSIONATE PURSUIT Flora Kidd
A DURABLE FIRE Robyn Donald
QUEEN OF THE CASTLE Nicola West
TWISTING SHADOWS Emma Darcy
A DEEPER DIMENSION Amanda Carpenter

Buy them from your usual paperback stockist, or write to: Mills & Boon Reader Service, P.O. Box 236, Thornton Rd, Croydon, Surrey CR9 3RU, England. Readers in South Africa-write to: Mills & Boon Reader Service of Southern Africa, Private Bag X3010, Randburg, 2125.

Mills & Boon

the rose of romance

ROMANCE

Variety is the spice of romance

Each month, Mills and Boon publish new romances. New stories about people falling in love. A world of variety in romance – from the best writers in the romantic world. Choose from these titles in February.

NEVER TRUST A STRANGER Kay Thorpe
COME LOVE ME Lilian Peake
CASTLE OF THE LION Margaret Rome
SIROCCO Anne Mather
TANGLE OF TORMENT Emma Darcy
A MISTAKE IN IDENTITY Sandra Field
RIDE THE WIND Yvonne Whittal
BACKFIRE Sally Wentworth
A RULING PASSION Daphne Clair
THE SILVER FLAME Margaret Pargeter
THE DUKE WORE JEANS Kay Clifford
THE PRICE OF FREEDOM Alison Fraser

On sale where you buy paperbacks. If you require further information or have any difficulty obtaining them, write to: Mills & Boon Reader Service, PO Box 236, Thornton Road, Croydon, Surrey CR9 3RU, England.

Mills & Boon

the rose of romance

Best Seller Romances

These best loved romances are back

Mills & Boon Best Seller Romances are the love stories that have proved particularly popular with our readers. These are the titles to look out for this month.

THE VINES IN SPLENDOUR
Helen Bianchin

SUMMER MAHOGANY
Janet Dailey

SWEET TORMENT
Flora Kidd

THE LONG SURRENDER
Charlotte Lamb

Buy them from your usual paperback stockist, or write to: Mills & Boon Reader Service, P.O. Box 236, Thornton Rd, Croydon, Surrey CR9 3RU, England. Readers in South Africa-write to: Mills & Boon Reader Service of Southern Africa, Private Bag X3010, Randburg 2125.

Mills & Boon

the rose of romance

Masquerade Historical Romances

From the golden days of romance

Picture the days of real romance – from the colourful courts of mediaeval Spain to the studied manners of Regency England. Masquerade Historical romances published by Mills & Boon vividly recreate the past. Look out for these superb new stories this month.

MISTRESS OF KOH-I-NOOR
Lynne Brooks

FIRST LOVE, LAST LOVE
Jessica Sayers

Buy them from your usual paperback stockist, or write to: Mills & Boon Reader Service, P.O. Box 236, Thornton Rd, Croydon, Surrey CR9 3RU, England. Readers in South Africa - write to: Mills & Boon Reader Service of Southern Africa, Private Bag X3010, Randburg, 2125.

Mills & Boon

the rose of romance

4 BOOKS FREE

Enjoy a Wonderful World of Romance...

Passionate and intriguing, sensual and exciting. A top quality selection of four Mills & Boon titles written by leading authors of Romantic fiction can be delivered direct to your door absolutely FREE!

Try these Four Free books as your introduction to Mills & Boon Reader Service. You can be among the thousands of women who enjoy six brand new Romances every month PLUS a whole range of special benefits.

- Personal membership card.
- Free monthly newsletter packed with recipes, competitions, exclusive book offers and a monthly guide to the stars.
- Plus extra bargain offers and big cash savings.

There is no commitment whatsoever, no hidden extra charges and your first parcel of four books is absolutely FREE!

Why not send for more details now? Simply complete and send the coupon to MILLS & BOON READER SERVICE, P.O. BOX 236, THORNTON ROAD, CROYDON, SURREY, CR9 3RU, ENGLAND. OR why not telephone us on 01-684 2141 and we will send you details about the Mills & Boon Reader Service Subscription Scheme – you'll soon be able to join us in a wonderful world of Romance.

Please note:– READERS IN SOUTH AFRICA write to Mills & Boon Ltd., Postbag X3010, Randburg 2125, S. Africa.

Please send me details of the Mills & Boon Reader Service Subscription Scheme.

NAME (Mrs/Miss) ______________________ EP6

ADDRESS ______________________

____

COUNTY/COUNTRY ______________________

POSTCODE ______________________

BLOCK LETTERS PLEASE